CREATIVE VICTORY

CREATIVE VICTORY

Reflections on the Process of Power from the Collected Works of Carlos Castaneda

Tomas

SAMUEL WEISER, INC.

York Beach, Maine

First published in 1995 by
Samuel Weiser Inc.
Box 612
York Beach, ME 03910-0612

Library of Congress Cataloging-in-Publication Data
Tomas.
    Creative victory : reflections on the process of power from the collected
works of carlos castaneda / Tomas.
        p. cm.
    1. Spiritual life. 2. Self-actualization (Psychology)--Religious aspects. 3.
Castaneda, Carlos, 1931- . 4. Juan, Don, 1891- . 5. Mythology, I. Title.
BL624.T65 1995
299'.7--dc20   95-10859
ISBN 0-87728-853-4   CIP
MG

Book design by Dizzy Fish Studios Inc.

Cover Art: *The Call of the Sea* Copyright © 1987 Daved Levitan.
Used by permission.

Typeset in 12 point Palatino

Printed in the United States of America

02 01 00 99 98 97 96 95
10 9 8 7 6 5 4 3 2 1

The paper in this publication meets the minimum requirements of
the American National Standard for Permanence of Paper for
Printed Library Materials Z39 .48-1984.

For all the seekers
on this marvelous Earth,
especially those who remain behind.

CONTENTS

PART TEN: THE PROMISE ALWAYS KEPT

PREFACE

My wife and I remain a couple in shock. In the five years since we first met the author of this book, our world has turned upside down in the most disturbing and invigorating of ways. We could never begin to describe the essence of our experience as caretakers of this material or our relationship with the man who brought us to it. He has overpowered us without a single touch, he has instructed us without a single lesson, he has empowered us with the simple emphasis of his words.

Whatever has happened (and is still happening) to us, we certainly don't understand it. We were simply an overworked pair of artists, newly arrived in a nice southern town. Soon after we got settled, we struck up a casual relationship with a charming Latin gentleman named Tomas. It was a friendship that developed slowly and remained relatively superficial for more than a year.

During that time, we worked with Tomas editing and visualizing a screenplay he had written. Our professional association was very pleasant, a fact that made it easy for us to establish a casual and comfortable friendship with him as well.

We appreciated Tomas as a person, but beyond that we really didn't give our budding relationship with him much thought. We were preoccupied at the time with the complexities of trying to adjust to our new home and work environment, and believed our friend was simply another artist like ourselves. We took him at face value for what he appeared to be, an interesting and talented man who took pleasure in discussing creative philosophy when the opportunity presented itself.

Looking back, we now know there was much more to Tomas and his work than we ever imagined. I don't want to say that he deceived us, but for more than a year this charming man kept the truly magical aspect of his character well concealed. Then one night Tomas opened the door to a part of himself that we never dreamed existed.

The series of events that followed this revelation took us unaware and set us on a path that changed our lives. Even so, they were part of a gradual process that crept up on us in the most innocent of ways. We just followed our hearts from day to day, until the fateful morning when we watched the life we knew unravel right before our eyes.

We now believe that this terrifying and empowering development was triggered in part by our involvement with Tomas' first book, a concordance to the collected works of a new-age author named Carlos Castaneda. That manuscript came to be called *The Promise of Power,* and the following portion of our foreword to that book describes how we met Tomas and became the enthusiastic caretakers of his first directory to the Toltec warriors' dialogue.

We are artists by trade, and as is the case with many of our professional colleagues, we have often found ourselves involved in situations that challenged our creativity in unexpected ways.

Four years ago, when we moved our small design studio to a coastal state, we began an association with a man who led us into such a creative endeavor, an undertaking that defied even our well-developed sense of the unexpected. This adventure involved a series of events that seem unbelievable in the retelling; a tale of power that led us to the day of this writing.

We have been privileged to edit and prepare this manuscript on behalf of a special friend of ours, a man we have come to know only as "Tomas." This delightful older gentleman was one of the first friends we made in our new seaside home, and for some unnamed reason we hit it off with him right away. Over the years we have spent many wonderful evenings discussing art and life with this captivating man, and even though we feel we know him well, circumstances have forced us to realize that we really don't know him at all.

Tomas is of Latin descent, an artist and writer by profession (although he has been reluctant to share a great deal of his other work with us). As near as we can tell, Tomas is in his 60s, even though he is much more vital than the average sexagenarian. Lean and dark-skinned, he is blessed with a very engaging smile.

Even though he has alluded to being a grandparent like us, Tomas has an impish, child-like quality which we find endearing in a most inexplicable way. So much so in fact, that my wife now calls this older man "Tommy" as an expression of her affection for his irrepressibly youthful qualities.

Our sporadic relationship with Tomas has been characterized by a series of inconsistencies. On one hand, he has been very open and friendly with us, but at the same time he has avoided revealing much of anything about himself or his family. He has been a frequent guest in our home, but he has never invited us to his house or even told us where he lives. He seems to be relatively well-fixed, but as far as we can tell, he has no telephone or car.

Beyond these superficial discrepancies, we have realized that Tomas' entire way of being is strangely contradictory. He appears to be old and young at the same time; innocent and playful in the midst of his obvious wisdom and sophistication. There is also an infectious dynamism about this man that invigorates us whenever we are around him. And yet in spite of his obvious energy, Tomas exudes an air of tranquility that is unlike anything we have ever experienced before.

Tomas is unique, and my wife and I have come to treasure his friendship dearly. In many ways we know Tomas' companionship was instrumental in helping us make the difficult adjustment to a new town, and yet for more than a year we took our pleasant relationship with him more or less for granted. Then one night everything changed.

During one of our occasional weekend chats, we happened to discover that Tomas had compiled a personal reference guide to the collected works of a well known new-age author. We learned about the existence of this catalog when the name of Carlos Castaneda came up in the course of conversation.

As a casual student of various spiritual writers, my wife was familiar with Castaneda's work, and that evening we happened to be discussing how she had introduced me to passages from *The Fire From Within* on our honeymoon. I told Tomas how I became intrigued with the story of a man who had jumped off a cliff and survived to tell about it, and how my interest had led me to read several of Carlos' books.

I was forced to admit, however, that despite my early enthusiasm, I had become frustrated with the Castaneda material. Although I enjoyed the lyrical narrative quality of the books, I found it difficult to get a handle on their underlying spiritual content. After reading three of them, I just couldn't seem to "get it," even though I had a clear intuitive sense that something tantalizing was mirrored in the pages of Carlos' work.

I commented that despite this vague intuition, my inability to connect with the essence of don Juan's teachings led me to abandon Castaneda's work for other more pressing matters. My wife agreed that she, too, had experienced difficulty distilling anything substantive from the numerous Carlos books that she had read. In her opinion, the essential themes of many other new age writings were much more accessible to the average reader.

Tomas took us off guard when he responded to our comments regarding our frustrations with the Castaneda books. He said he knew exactly what we were talking about because he had been a devoted student of Carlos Castaneda's writings for many years. Tomas said that even after reading the collected Castaneda books countless times, he had also found the essence of this very abstract material difficult to grasp.

My wife and I were both a little surprised by Tomas' revelation. He had never impressed us as the studious type, much less as the kind of person who would dedicate himself to the writings of a controversial new-age guru. But our surprise became astonishment when Tomas went on to tell us that his personal study of Castaneda's work had led him to compile a complex series of notes and references on the Castaneda material.

We were actually somewhat skeptical as Tomas explained how, over of period of many years, he had assembled a massive reference guide to the Toltec warriors' dialogue; a catalog of sorts that allowed him to cross-reference and easily access thousands of isolated references scattered throughout the eight Castaneda books in print. He told us he had prepared his reference guide as a personal exercise designed to help him access the underlying essence of what he called "nagualism."

Once we determined that Tomas wasn't joking with us about his catalog, my wife and I immediately became interested in finding out more about it. Months later, when we finally convinced him to share some small portions of it with us, we were amazed at the intuitive and organizational clarity he had brought to the Castaneda material. It only took a brief review of his work for us to realize that Tomas was much more of a scholar than we had ever suspected.

It was very clear that our casual friend had accomplished something remarkable. He had created a reference work that rendered an intimidating body of very abstract material much more understandable. To our minds, his efforts paralleled those of Marianne Williamson (an insightful author who had distilled concepts from a little-known treatise called *A Course In Miracles* and published them as a national bestseller titled *A Return to Love*).

After studying his notes in depth, we began urging Tomas to consider publishing his work as well. My wife and I guessed (based on our own experience) that many casual Castaneda readers would find xvi • CREATIVE VICTORY

Tomas' work of interest, and that a book based on his catalog would be a tremendous reference guide for anyone interested in exploring the spirit of the teachings of don Juan in more detail.

It occurred to us that perhaps the Castaneda material would benefit from the same kind of distillation as *A Course in Miracles* . We felt that many people must have been tantalized by the same magical thread we had encountered in the Carlos books, and we were sure that our friend's catalog would make this unspoken core much more accessible to the average reader.

Our theory led us to become keenly focused on the inspirational potential of Tomas' work. We came to believe his catalog was a diamond in the rough; that once polished and presented, it would bring great additional clarity to a body of knowledge that had intrigued (and probably somewhat frustrated) millions of readers all around the world.

But despite our enthusiasm for publishing his "catalog of one thousand secrets," we quickly learned Tomas had a very different opinion of our idea. He vehemently disagreed with our well-intentioned suggestion and refused to even consider publishing his notes, arguing that his catalog had been prepared as a personal task of learning, and not as a project for publication.

For months, Tomas remained adamant that creating a book from his notes would taint the very personal nature of his work and produce a most undesirable series of "first attention" consequences. He simply refused to involve himself and his catalog in the contractual, financial, and ego-related issues of new age book authorship.

But much to our own surprise, my wife and I would not take no for an answer. We are normally not pushy people, but our intuition kept nagging us about this project, and so we kept pestering Tomas, hoping that he might eventually change his mind. Finally, after months of additional coaxing, we were able to break through and convince our friend that a book based on his notes could be published without the first attention consequences that so concerned him.

The solution we proposed was simple. It called for us to act as Tomas' personal representatives on the project. We would handle everything in his behalf, including all necessary dealings with attorneys, agents, and publishers. We also assured Tomas that we would gladly do all the design, editing, and mechanical assembly work on the manuscript, since this was something we already did as part of our professional repertoire.

This suggestion eventually turned the tide in our favor, and months later, Tomas finally gave us his enthusiastic go-ahead with one all-important condition. He insisted that we coordinate all aspects of the publishing process without his direct involvement, and above all else, that we keep his identity secret.

Remaining anonymous has always been of paramount importance to Tomas. As he explained it to us, without his anonymity, he would be unable to his maintain his "equilibrium" with respect to the catalog he had created. He said that in order to preserve the spirit of his efforts, the private nature of his learning task had to be preserved.

We never fully understood what Tomas meant by all this, but we respected his point of view just the same. Since the day we first became his representatives, my wife and I have done everything in our power to honor our friend's wish for anonymity. This has not been difficult, since even we know precious little about Tomas in the first place.

Before work on *The Promise of Power* was complete, Tomas moved away from the town where we lived and worked at the time. The last communication we had from him was his hand-written prelude for *The Promise of Power* (which he left for us to find on our doorstep).

After Tomas' abrupt departure, we didn't hear from him again for some time. Then, after many months, he began contacting us with drafts and revisions for several other writing projects he had in progress. He told us he was pleased with the way we had handled *The Promise of Power,* and requested that we continue to work with him on several other manuscripts that he was in the process of preparing.

We have agreed to continue acting as Tomas' representatives, even though we have plenty of legitimate reasons to justify walking away from this very stressful responsibility. At the time of this writing, our lives are in shambles and Tomas continues to become steadily more removed from us, frustrating us with his unavailability and his unwillingness to deal with us in a normal way.

More than five years after our first meeting, we now often awake from a fitful night wishing we'd never become involved with our Latin friend to begin with. But then the truth bubbles back up within us and we regain our courage. For on the deepest level we have no doubt that some positive momentum is carrying us. We have to believe that the process unfolding around Tomas and his manuscripts is more than it appears and that it is up to us to trust in the mystery of it all.

But in spite of our heartfelt intuition, it hasn't been easy for us to sustain the belief that everything is happening as it should. The familiar structure of the life we knew has fallen away, leaving us dumfounded and afraid. The challenges of our current circumstance have left us naked in a world we do not recognize, with only the faintest glimmer of a distant light to guide us. It is the beacon of an intangible creative victory that waits for us, an impossible contradiction that hovers silently between the terror and the wonder of the days ahead.

The concept of *creative victory* has intrigued us ever since we first heard about it from Tomas a number of years ago. It became one of our favorite topics of conversation, and we incorporated many applications of this powerful concept into both our personal and professional lives. In fact, we were so touched by the idea that we even established a Creative Victory Apprenticeship program at our small design studio, involving student interns from a local design school.

At one point (when we thought we would not hear from Tomas again), we went so far as to consider writing some kind of a treatise on creative victory ourselves. But before we could find time to initiate the project, Tomas forwarded us the first draft of this book. We were disappointed at first (for all the wrong reasons of course), but after reading Tomas' manuscript, we realized that we would never have been able to do the subject justice.

This book is a series of essays on the process of power as it is described within the collected works of Carlos Castaneda.

The Teachings of Don Juan
A Separate Reality
Journey To Ixtlan
Tales of Power
The Second Ring of Power
The Eagle's Gift
The Fire From Within
The Power of Silence
The Art of Dreaming

It will be next to impossible for the reader to make sense of *Creative Victory* without a perspective on the concepts and terminology contained within the nine books listed above. Tomas refers to this body of work as the Toltec warriors' dialogue (or the written record of nagualism), and has prepared a concordance called *The Promise of Power* as an aid in accessing its complexities. We have convinced the author to include a brief glossary of terms at the end of this book to help readers unfamiliar with the Castaneda material to get their bearings, but for those interested in further study, this abbreviated listing cannot substitute for a thorough exploration of the Toltec warriors' dialogue itself.

My wife and I are especially excited that this manuscript is being published. We believe in *Creative Victory,* and in the intent of the man who left it in our care. We see this work as a powerful companion to *The Promise of Power* and as a sincere deposit to what the Toltecs call "the account of the spirit of man."*

In keeping with the author's instructions, we have endeavored to make our own contribution to this special undertaking. We have done our best to edit and prepare this manuscript and only hope that, in some small way, our intent will add to the impeccable momentum of Tomas' work.

Dizzy Fish Studios

---

*Tomas has always intended that his books be used as reference guides to the Toltec warriors' dialogue, and not as stand-alone commentaries. In keeping with that intent, we urge you to use this book (in conjunction with his earlier *The Promise of Power*) as a tool to explore the nine volumes of the Toltec warriors' dialogue. It is our understanding that Tomas has prepared *Creative Victory* as a companion to *The Promise of Power,* both of which are intended to serve as informational and intuitive directories to the powerful written record of nagualism. Concepts and terms mentioned in *Creative Victory* can be located as alphabetical entries in the "Catalog of One Thousand Secrets" section of *The Promise of Power.* These entries will in turn lead the reader to specific selected references from the Castaneda books themselves. (See *The Promise of Power* for information on the specific editions of the Castaneda books to which the concordance is referenced.)

FOREWORD

A FOOL'S DEPOSIT

I am a fool in the hands of power. I am unable to explain why my life has transformed itself in the ways it has, I can only laugh with my friends, the trees, and contemplate the impossibility of it all.

In an earlier book, *The Promise of Power,* I described how I came to the writings of Carlos Castaneda and the Toltec warriors' dialogue. I have no particular qualifications as a commentator on this material, but I now find myself compelled to participate in the preparation of this and other commentaries, nonetheless. This book is an extension of my unlikely travels with power. Beyond that, there is little I can say, because there are no words in my first attention vocabulary to describe the essence of my experience.

I cannot categorize the process I've undergone in preparing this book as "writing" in the traditional sense. And even though I have played a part in the creation of a number of manuscripts based on the published works of Carlos Castaneda, I know that I have merely acted as a facilitator for materials that were otherwise destined to come to the fore through me.

I say this because my first attention self has not been responsible for consciously creating this or any of the other manuscripts I have been involved with. As the Toltecs tell us, true *creativity* does not belong to the tonal, it springs from the incomprehensible nagual.

Knowing this, I must accept the events surrounding the assembly of these books as part of an incomprehensible mystery, a mystery that is clearly beyond my intellectual capacities. *Impeccability* dictates that I simply accept my role as intermediary with the humility of the fool.

I am grateful to the spirit for the challenges of my life and offer this book as an expression of my gratitude. As with *The Promise of Power,* I intend for this work to stand as a payment to what the Toltecs call "the account of the spirit of man." Don Juan tells us that this meager account is always in need of deposits, and that no matter how we choose to add to that ledger, any form of *impeccable* payment is always enough.

Giving back to this depleted account is one way of repaying the benevolence of those who have touched us throughout our lives. I can only hope that the deposits of this fool will account in some small part for favors received from others on the way to *power's promise.*

THE BEACON OF NAGUALISM

Nagualism is the term most often used to describe the knowledge of the Toltec warrior-sorcerer. I have *seen* that this knowledge represents a beacon of return to the unalterable abstract, a light to guide us back to *power's promise.*

The warriors' dialogue is the written record of this knowledge; a prism that reflects the beacon of nagualism into the innermost depths of our being. Once the radiance of those magical insights has touched our lives, we find ourselves changing in ways that are not comprehensible to our physical senses or our rational minds.

I *have* to believe that the world is in the midst of a revolution of return to the essence of our being. I also *have* to believe that the Toltec warriors' dialogue has a part to play in this spiritual evolution. The beacon of the nagual shines incomprehensibly from the pages of Carlos Castaneda's books, providing mankind with a universal message of hope, empowerment, and transcendency. Somehow in keeping with the unfathomable designs of power, my fool's awareness has positioned itself to reflect that gentle light as well.

THE FLAW WITH WORDS

History has shown that the human race has a nearly inexhaustible desire to render comprehensible that which is incomprehensible. Since the beginning of time, men and women have struggled to express what they can only intuit with their hearts, but no matter how eloquent their descriptions and their stories, the essence of the inexplicable has always remained beyond the scope of words.

From the Toltec perspective, this is the way it always must be, and so it is not surprising to find that the warrior-sorcerers of don Juan's lineage also felt compelled to discuss their transcendental experiences in the most cogent terms possible. In fact, it is the descriptive account of those discussions (as chronicled in the nine books by Carlos Castaneda) that makes up the available written record of Toltec knowledge.

What is interesting about this particular attempt to describe the indescribable, is that it specifically addresses the inadequacy of language as part of its spiritual account. As contradictory as it seems, the Toltecs actually preface their remarks by urging us to understand that true knowledge exists independent of language altogether.

Those of us attempting to access the essence of nagualism must accept an outrageous premise; even though the teachings of don Juan are now available in print, the silent knowledge that underlies those teachings remains completely beyond the power of the written word. The Toltecs insist that anything truly "of the spirit" must be actualized as a personal experience rather than simply written or talked about as an intellectual concept.

Understanding and accepting this contradiction is one of the fundamental aspects of the *preamble of power.* Even though human beings have been conditioned from birth to believe that they can access anything through language, warriors intuit the inherent flaw with words; they force us to feel enlightened when we are not!

It is impossible to explore the Toltec experience without transcending this insidious and fatal flaw with language. We must respect the unfathomable nature of the mysterious universe by rejecting the ludicrous notion that simply reading and thinking about nagualism will eventually lead us to a direct and silent understanding of the abstract.

Knowledge and power are unfathomable by nature, and when they are acquired, they are acquired inexplicably. No initiate in the world of power can ever hope to explain the essence of silent knowledge, not don Juan, not Carlos Castaneda and certainly not myself. The most any of us can do is engage in a warriors' dialogue, an intellectual exercise that mirrors the beacon of the nagual within the contradictory framework of the spoken and written word.

In her book, *Being-In-Dreaming,* Florinda Donner reminds us that the personal exploration of alternate views of reality is essentially an intellectual exercise that, in itself, does not have the capacity to change us. The written record of nagualism presents us with just such an alternate view, and we must continually remind ourselves that true enlightenment is the result of *impeccable* action and experience, not scholarly pursuits and intellectual mind play.

Don Juan tells us that the theoretical warrior is really no warrior at all. In order to really change anything in our world, we must carry the spirit of nagualism beyond the realm of talking and thinking into the realm of action!

The pursuit of *power's promise* is the most complex and rewarding endeavor imaginable and it all begins with the transcendence of the flaw with words. We must not allow the false clarity of an intellectual exercise to imprison us. Instead we must actualize the road to our unlimited potential by transforming the intruiging concepts of theoretical nagualism into a life of empirical warriorship and sorcery!

A TIME TO ACT

Warriors live in the moment of now and now is the time to act! Sooner or later we must step beyond the warriors' dialogue and exchange our tidy arrangement of knowledge for a life of *impeccable* action! Sooner or later the intellectual and intuitive *preamble of power* must give way to a personal and empirical process! Sooner or later we must claim our knowledge of mysteries by experiencing the significant movement of the assemblage point!

As warriors, we face the contradictions of knowledge by daring to act! We assume responsibility for our own energetic resources while releasing ourselves to power. And through our actions we learn to balance the forces of warriorship and sorcery, realizing in the process that our *creative victory* emerges from the heart of this awesome dichotomy.

The way of the warrior-sorcerer requires that we *rest* until we can pit the contradictions of knowledge one against the other in an *impeccable* search for the truth. There is nothing logical about this unfathomable course of action, simply because there is nothing rational or explicable about power to begin with.

No man or woman can map the path of knowledge or predict the way in which a warrior's *victory* will be won. The rule dictates that we must take our place among the unfathomable mysteries of the universe by simply regarding ourselves as one.

Power is, and power moves. These are the only things that any of us can know for sure. But for some of us, the theoretical realization of this truth is not enough. Instead of just thinking and talking about the incomprehensible nature of the universe, warriors act to gather themselves until the reality of power and its movements have become a part of their personal and direct experience!

T.W.W.

Part One
Introduction

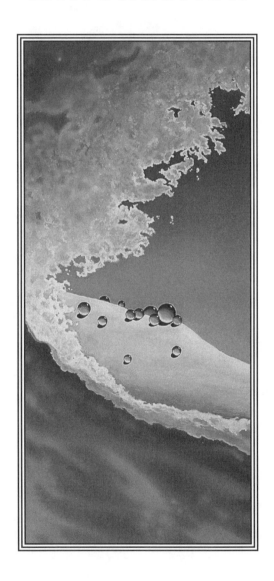

THE MAGIC
OF NAGUALISM

A MESSAGE FOR ALL MANKIND

The true magic of nagualism is that it entices us back to the abstract through a message of universal hope, empowerment, and transcendency. This message is grounded in the universal covenant that flows from the essential and incomprehensible relationship between the luminous beings and power itself. This is the unalterable *promise of power*, and it can be summarized as follows:

> *One day each and every human being*
> *will return to the abstract in a state of total awareness.*

The *promise of power* is an expression of the essential and incomprehensible connection between power and the luminous beings. The *promise of power* is not an imagined or theoretical contract, it can be verified by anyone with the personal power to *see*.

The *promise of power* is the beacon of the nagual, a tantalizing covenant that establishes the nature and purpose of the warriors' journey of return to the abstract. In the world of the first attention, the potential realization of this promise expresses itself as a magical portal of power, otherwise known as the Toltec path of knowledge.

THE PREAMBLE OF POWER

The Toltec path of knowledge begins with a manifestation of the spirit that opens the existence of power's promise to the heart and mind of a given individual. Under the appropriate circumstances, this perceptual breakthrough leads to the internalization of a series of ultra personal insights regarding the nature of the energetic universe and the essential and incomprehensible connection between the luminous beings and power itself. *Dreaming* has lead me to call the assimilation of these critical insights the *preamble of power.*

The *preamble of power* is a direct manifestation of the spirit, and as such, it has the power to change our lives if we allow it to do so. But recognizing the bird of *freedom,* is only the first step on the Toltec path of knowledge. Having identified our most magical opportunity, it is up to us to act.

THE PROCESS OF POWER

The Toltecs have shown us that in order to change any-thing, we must carry the spirit of *power's preamble* beyond the realm of intellect and intuition into the realm of action and personal experience! Thoughts and beliefs must be supplanted by the empirical practice of warriorship and sorcery!

Nagualism builds on the *preamble of power* by providing mankind with a portal of return to *power's promise.* The process of power is the incomprehensible dynamic that moves human beings through that opening to *freedom* with their entire bodies. This process is characterized by the movement of the assemblage point from the position of normal awareness to the position of total awareness. Unlike *power's preamble*, it is a living course of action that transcends words all together and vaults the warrior directly into the unfathomable world of intent.

THE ULTERIOR ARRANGEMENT
OF A FOOL'S DIRECTORIES

M any years ago I began assembling a concordance to the Toltec warriors' dialogue as a personal exercise of learning. Over time, that cataloging effort unwittingly evolved into a book called *The Promise of Power*, an informational and intuitive directory that focuses on the written record of nagualism and the portal of return to *power's promise.*

Creative Victory is also an informational and intuitive directory to the Toltec warriors' dialogue, with one very significant difference. Instead of just focusing on the way that warriors have thought and talked about the details of the path of knowledge, *Creative Victory* is a call to action for those who have been touched by the manifestation of the spirit.

In keeping with the Toltec tradition, the ulterior arrangement of *The Promise of Power* and *Creative Victory* mirrors the essential progression of the Toltec path of knowledge. The realm of the tonal must open and embrace the realm of the nagual!

By this I mean that talking and thinking must always give way to *impeccable* action! The intellectual and intuitive exercises of theoretical nagualism must transform themselves into the practicing arts of the warrior-sorcerer! Instead of capturing us in a manageable web of language, the tantalizing power of the warriors' dialogue must spur each of us to initiate our own empirical *process of power!*

REDEFINING VICTORY

P ower has lead me to use the term *creative victory* as a synonym for one aspect of the *process of power.* By definition, this unconditional form of *victory* differs greatly from the term as it is used by the average person in the perspective of the first attention.

In the Toltec context, *victory* must be thought of as an intangible process rather than a tangible reward, an ongoing state of being rather than a static goal. For the warrior-sorcerer, *victory* is a state of joyful balance and transcendence, not conditional superiority over people and petty circumstances.

In the mysterious world of power, the warriors' *victory* must be redefined as the harmony of thought and action, the equanimity of the tonal and the nagual. *Creative victory* is a magical process of renewal that washes over us as we balance the *doing* and *not-doing* of warriorship and sorcery.

WHAT MANKIND NEEDS NOW

D on Juan tells us exactly what we require most in the midst of our modern world. He contends that we must de-emphasize our attachment to the world of solid objects and allow magic to get hold of us instead. This simple change of emphasis has the power to banish doubts from our minds, and once those doubts have been erased, all things are possible, including a return to the abstract in a state of total awareness.

This is the Toltecs' simple and empowering advice for all mankind. In order to accomplish our journey of return, we do not need more technology or greater self-involvement. On the contrary, what we require is to shift our emphasis away from those very things. In order to find *freedom*, we must detach ourselves from our description of the world and learn the secrets of the assemblage point!

Don Juan tells us that it is through this simple change of emphasis, not through methods, that we will best be assisted in the attainment of our ultimate *creative victory*. Many (in fact most) things remain beyond us on the inexplicable road to power, but assuming personal responsibility for the emphasis of our lives is one thing that warriors can control.

AN IMPECCABLE EMPHASIS

In the flurry of normal awareness, most human beings turn a blind eye to the mysterious realm of intent and to the glimmer of power's universal promise. The misguided emphasis of the first attention focuses average people so completely on a single familiar expression of the abstract that they remain unaware of their inconceivable potential.

An all-consuming self-absorption depletes our natural energy until we can recognize nothing beyond the obvious conditions of the world of solid objects. The promise of our most magical opportunity dances before us every day, but we are much too involved with our own self-reflection to respond.

But not so the warriors of the Toltec tradition. We train ourselves to release the things that once held us prisoner in the world of the tonal, and open ourselves to the magic of *power's promise*. We commit ourselves to a new and *impeccable* emphasis by gathering our energetic resources and declaring war on that portion of the personal self that deprives us of our power.

THE KEY TO VICTORY

*R*esting is a primary focus of this manuscript because it is the key to the *process of power*. When we *rest*, we access and conserve the invisible energetic resources that are our birthright; we empower ourselves in a way that is real and yet incomprehensible to our first attention senses.

The warriors who *rest* are simply individuals who have declared war on their own self-importance and who have succeeded in drawing energy from that struggle. In Toltec terms, they are *impeccable* warriors, warriors who have gathered and re-channeled their own personal power.

Very few of us are born with a natural inclination to *rest* in the Toltec sense of the word. Such individuals would require a natural sobriety and an unusually "selfless" perspective on the world. The reality for most human beings is that we are trained to focus completely on our own self-image and the "conditional" solidity of the prevailing social order.

Don Juan tells us that the only way to expand ourselves beyond the unshakable finality of the world we know is to conserve the energy that we normally pour into keeping the assemblage point fixed in its habitual position. Warriors know that the only way to gather this energy and tip the perceptual scales is to live *impeccably* (or *rest* and rechannel our natural energetic resources).

In this sense, *resting* is the key to our unlimited potential, because it is the single conscious pivot-point on the incomprehensible path of knowledge. Most everything else warrior-sorcerers do is beyond their waking control, so choosing to *rest* is a deliberate act of unparalleled importance.

The struggle to consciously shift our personal emphasis is unimaginably difficult, because the momentum of the prevailing social order and our own self-indulgent habits give us every conceivable excuse not to do so. In order to actualize our intent to *rest*, we must accomplish the extraordinary. Not only must we turn our backs on the emphasis of the modern world, we must also shift ourselves away from the self-involved focus that has consumed us since the moment of our birth.

From the Toltec point of view, nothing on the path of knowledge is more important than *impeccability,* and *dreaming* has lead me to equate the word *rest* with that Toltec term. As warriors, it is our responsibility to actualize the beginnings of the incomprehensible *process of power* by becoming the warriors who *rest.*

FLOWING WITH AN AFFIRMATION

I try to remember from my waking perspective that I will never be anything more than just a fool. My first attention self is stubborn and tenacious to an incalculable degree, and I must struggle constantly to maintain a viewpoint beyond the world of circumstance and solid objects. One thing that has helped me in my efforts is the consistent use of personal affirmations as part of my daily life.

Such affirming personal statements are common in spiritual traditions the world over, and several can be found in the Toltec warriors' dialogue as well. These special reminders are marvelous tools in the conscious transformation of the personal facade, and my own experience has shown that "talking to oneself" in this way can produce remarkable results.

Power has led me to many personal affirmations during the course of my life, and one of the most meaningful has been *An Affirmation for the Warrior Who*

Rests. This verse was first published as part of *The Promise of Power,* and has now evolved into the *dreaming* outline for this manuscript on *creative victory.**

*The reader will note that the arrangement of this manuscript flows directly from *An Affirmation for the Warrior Who Rests.* Each pair of lines from the affirmation is the focus of a short three-part essay. These brief compositions are in turn grouped together in sets of three to form nine larger sections that mirror the nine stanzas of this affirming statement.

AN AFFIRMATION FOR
THE WARRIOR WHO RESTS

*The promise of power
is the promise always kept.*

*The promise of power
is made to the warrior who rests.*

*All things come
to the warrior who rests.*

I am the warrior who rests.
I am the warrior impeccable.

I am the warrior who rests.
I am the warrior empowered.

I am the warrior who rests.
I am the warrior proactive.

I am the warrior who rests.
I have learned to protect myself.

I am the warrior who rests.
I have learned to nurture myself.

I am the warrior who rests.
I have learned to love myself.

I am the warrior who rests.
I am the warrior who breathes deeply.

I am the warrior who rests.
I am the warrior who sees clearly.

I am the warrior who rests.
I am the warrior who chooses well.

I am the warrior who rests.
I have learned to conserve my own energy.

I am the warrior who rests.
I have learned to be in touch with my own strength.

I am the warrior who rests.
I have learned to direct my life with
my intuition and my intent.

I am the warrior who rests.
I have balanced sobriety and abandon.

I am the warrior who rests.
I have shattered the mirror of my own
self-reflection.

I am the warrior who rests.
I have transformed my own facade.

I am the warrior who rests.
I have prepared myself for dreaming.

I am the warrior who rests.
I have joyfully walked my personal path with heart.

I am the warrior who rests.
I have found peace in my creative victory,
a victory without glory or reward.

I am the warrior who rests.
I have learned the gentle art of letting go.

I am the warrior who rests.
I have learned there is no substitute for resting.

I am the warrior who rests.
I have learned that resting is the key
to my unlimited potential.

*All things come
to the warrior who rests.*

*And all things become nothing
for the warrior who waits.*

*The promise of power
is the promise always kept.*

Part Two
The Promise Made

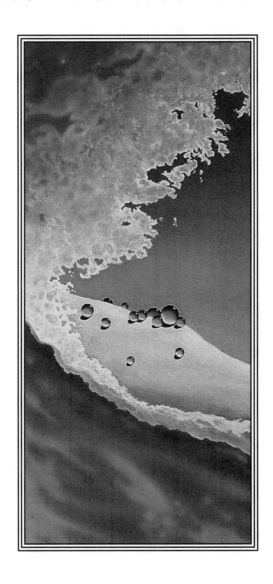

THE PROMISE
OF POWER

> ## The promise of power
> ## is the promise always kept

THE PROMISE

The *promise of power* is a beacon of return in the prevailing darkness of the age of the self. It is the glimmer of mankind's unlimited potential, shining brightly for us from the furthermost reaches of the spirit's infinite design.

The movements of power are beyond the mechanical grasp of any human being, and those rhythms reflect themselves in the world of the first attention as unfathomable mysteries and glaring contradictions. No matter how we struggle to make sense of these complexities, the designs of the spirit are not for us to know.

Power's promise lies at the heart of this unfathomable mystery, and as such, it is characterized by a similar incongruity. Although universal and unalterable in its scope and application, no one can predict how the *promise of power* will translate itself to the fate of any man or woman on Earth.

As warriors, we acquiesce to this contradiction with respect and humility. We accept that we are in the hands of a mystery beyond understanding and that we can best respect the enigma of power by actualizing an attitude of *impeccable* release. This empowering sense of detachment is eloquently described in the words of the Toltec warrior's formula:

> *I am already given to the power that rules my fate.*
> *And I cling to nothing,*
> *so that I will have nothing to defend.*
> *I have no thoughts so I will see.*
> *I fear nothing, so I will remember myself.*
> *Detached and at ease,*
> *I will dart past the Eagle to be free.*

But the warriors' acquiescence is not total or absolute, for it too must reflect the contradictory essence of power's incomprehensible designs. As travelers on the path of knowledge, we know that abandonment and release must be balanced with *impeccability* and the sober assumption of personal responsibility. The ultimate journey of return cannot be accomplished without equal measures of both sobriety and abandon artfully blended in a state of perfect balance.

We achieve this harmony as warrior-sorcerers by hovering delicately between the poles of a staggering contradiction; we balance our sense of abandon to power with the sober conservation of our most precious energetic resources. As true abstract warriors, we strive relentlessly to reconnect ourselves with intent, not by wrestling with the mechanical details of our destiny, but by endeavoring to travel an *impeccable* road wherever power leads us.

The *promise of power* is a promise made to all men and women as luminous beings. It is an unwavering constant that connects the whole of humanity to an unalterable reality beyond the world of solid objects. No matter how different the individual circumstances of our lives may appear to be, each of us is universally blessed by the implications of the same covenant of awareness, a universal and undeniable promise that power always keeps.

THE BIRD OF FREEDOM

T he shimmering beacon of *power's promise* tantalizes each of us on a hidden intuitive level, enticing us to initiate a personal journey of return to the abstract. Unfortunately, the human race has become conditioned to ignore these persistent glimmerings of the nagual. The complexities of the first attention keep most people so completely focused on a single familiar expression of the abstract that they remain lost in the midst of all their *doings.*

The only thing that most men and women perceive is the boundaries of a universe that they themselves have created, a world of solid objects, a world of the tonal. The majority of human beings remain imprisoned for a lifetime within the secure limits of that familiar world, never expanding themselves beyond the perceptual barrier of their own making.

It is an all-consuming sense of self that separates us from power, draining our available energy and surrounding us with the mirror of our own self-reflection. Magic leaps and dances before us every day, but we are too self-involved and too drained of power to recognize its presence.

We know that in order to come to knowledge, we must emerge from this self-reflective tunnel into the unimaginable expanse of the unknown and the unknowable. We must expand our perception beyond our conditional expectations by allowing ourselves to let go of the things that keep us prisoners in the world of the tonal.

As warriors of the Toltec tradition, we gather our energy and open ourselves to the light of *power's promise.* We release ourselves to the impossible prospect that there is an avenue of power that can return us *victorious* to the spirit.

The promise of such a miraculous triumph is the beacon of nagualism and the essence of the warriors' path of knowledge. The Toltecs have *seen* that every human being on Earth has a chance to have a chance, that each of us has the hidden capacity to realize an ultimate *creative victory.* This magical doorway of return is visualized throughout the warriors' dialogue as the metaphor of the bird of *freedom.*

The Toltecs say that this mysterious bird soars silently over all mankind, carrying with it an awareness of *power's promise.* The shadow of this awesome creature glides over each and every one of us, bringing universal hope and purpose to anyone prepared to recognize its presence through the edifice of intent.

Once perceived, the bird of *freedom* pauses for a moment in its flight, and it is then as individuals that we must choose. We may let the bird fly by or we may summon the courage to follow. If we choose to stay, the bird of *freedom* soars on, never to circle back. If we choose to follow, we set ourselves on the incomprehensible road to warriorship and sorcery.

And yet as with everything else on the mysterious path of knowledge, this Toltec metaphor is characterized by a baffling contradiction. Warriors know in spite of everything, that it is impossible for anyone to really "choose" warriorship, just as it is foolish to assign superiority to one choice over another. We are all in the hands of power and there can be no categorical right or wrong to our decision, however we may choose.

Those who *see*, understand that everything is equal and unimportant in the sphere of the tonal. Each of us is bound by the intricacies of our own fate. Nothing can change the fact that the *promise of power* remains forever constant, whether we accompany the bird of *freedom* or whether we choose to remain behind.

CHOOSING WARRIORSHIP

C hoosing warriorship is really not a choice at all. Even though we may delude ourselves into believing it is possible to understand and control a decision to follow the bird of *freedom*, that choice is merely another reflection of a mystery beyond our conscious control. It is power that leads us to the path of knowledge and the most any of us can ever do is acquiesce to its designs.

Seeing enables warriors to understand that decisions really don't belong to the world of the tonal. Human beings don't control their choices in the way the description of the world trains them to believe they do. Decisions belong to the nagual, where the concepts of control and reason have no meaning. As human beings who walk the earth, we choose and yet we do not choose. This is another fundamental contradiction of the warriors' path of knowledge.

From the Toltec perspective, it simply is not possible to "choose" to access knowledge, nor is it possible to turn away when the spirit decides to step to the fore. The business of coming to power is simply not a *doing* that can be manipulated. Warriors understand this and approach the path of knowledge as an incomprehensible *not-doing*. Rather than struggling to gain mechanical control over their avenue to power, warriors command the essence of their travels by not controlling anything.

In this sense, choosing warriorship is more an act of unconditional release than an act of conditional control. The abstract order of knowledge is beyond the grasp of any man or woman and warriors free themselves by accepting this fact with sobriety and ultimate humility. Power is and power moves. These are the only things we know for sure on the road to *power's promise.*

THE WARRIOR
WHO RESTS

> *The promise of power*
> *is made to the warrior who rests.*

THE MYSTERY OF RESTING

The *promise of power* is made to the warriors who *rest* because power and *impeccability* reinforce themselves. Although *resting* appears to be a conditional concept that produces predictable results, nothing could be further from the truth. Like everything else in our mysterious world, *resting* is actually an incomprehensible reflection of the nagual, and as a result, there is no simple formula for the way that *impeccability* leads to *power's promise*.

Those of us intent on traveling the road to power must accept this fundamental premise and learn to trust in what we cannot know. We can commit ourselves to a life of *rest*, but beyond that courageous act there is little else we can consciously control. The designs of power are not predictable, and we can be certain that the path of knowledge will always evolve unimaginably before our eyes.

There is no way to know what is in store for us along the road to *victory*. The only clue the Toltecs give us is that the key to our inner pathway lies hidden in the maze of our personal choices and the things to which we give our energetic emphasis.

THE WARRIORS' WAY OF HELPING

D on Juan tells us that what mankind needs now is assistance in becoming reconnected with the abstract. He also contends that if this assistance materializes, it will not come in the form of traditional instructional methods, but as the simple awareness that each of us has the power to redirect the emphasis of our lives.

This emphatic shift centers on the way we must act to re-prioritize our individual sense of self. As children of the tonal, we are trained to exalt the personal self above all else and make it the center of our waking world. This common form of self worship results in the consumption of all our available energy, leaving us deprived of the personal power necessary to accomplish a journey of return. It is only when we change our emphasis and direct ourselves away from self-reflection that the doorway to *power's promise* begins to open,

Don Juan offers a form of Toltec assistance just by advising us of the critical need to curtail self-importance. Strangely enough, the mere articulation of this advice is an apparent contradiction, because as a warrior-sorcerer-seer, don Juan was not a believer in "help" as we traditionally define it.

Deliberate intervention in the lives of others is not viewed by the Toltecs as being help at all. Their *seeing* has shown them that conscious and conditional acts of interference are mere indulgences of the helper's misdirected sense of self-importance. Don Juan's comments about the snail on the sidewalk or the way Carlos helped Pablito at the moment of their jump into the abyss are perfect examples of this Toltec perspective.

In keeping with his own silent knowledge, don Juan always opted not to meddle, thereby allowing for the emergence of the warrior spirit in those who he encountered. As a nagual, he knew that to intervene indiscriminately in the lives of others is to arrogantly assume to know what is best for them. No true warrior would never disrespect the incomprehensible designs of power in such a way.

For this reason, it is unlikely that a true Toltec seer would intervene in the life of even a single individual (unless specifically directed to do so by power itself). With this in mind, we must ask why the Toltecs would risk intervening in the lives of every Castaneda reader.

Don Juan answers this question by making one clear exception to his rule about assisting others. He contends that the only way one human being can truly help another is by making that person aware of the need to curtail self-importance. From the Toltec perspective, this is the only kind of "help" that is genuine and real.

I have *dreamed* that one of the primary purposes of the Toltec warriors' dialogue is to assist mankind by commenting on the fundamental importance of selflessness. No one can anticipate how the empowering message of nagualism will eventually impact the human race. The Toltec warriors' dialogue may find a way to assist mankind's spiritual evolution, or it may not. But whatever happens, it is of no particular concern to los nuevos videntes. They know without a doubt that the intricacies of such a complex issue remain solely in the hands of power.

THE WARRIOR AFFIRMED

*A*n *Affirmation for the Warrior Who Rests* is simply a reminder of the ever-present opportunity that power gives us to change our critical emphasis. Its nine stanzas represent an unstructured outline of the *process of power*, a personal affirmation that reflects the Toltecs' way of giving back to what they refer to as "the account of the spirit of man."

Unfortunately, this simple affirmation has no particular meaning for most human beings. But for the warrior, the spirit of these words is paramount because it echoes our magical "chance to have a chance," our opportunity to accept the *impeccable* help that don Juan and his Toltec predecessors have made available through the written record of nagualism.

What we choose to do with our minimal chance is up to us. When the shadow of the bird of *freedom* glides across our shoulder, we can choose to stay or we can choose to follow. We can keep the challenges of warriorship at arm's length, or we can accept the struggle of an *impeccable* life as the Toltecs suggest.

Don Juan tells us that eternity is all around us, and that any given moment can become eternity if we use it to take the totality of ourselves forever in any direction. Accepting the responsibility for finding our way to the impossibility of such a moment is the essence of the warrior's way of being.

As warriors, we cannot ignore the opportunity to return in full awareness to the eternity from whence we came. Following the designs of the spirit, we will accept the spirit of the Toltecs' unconditional assistance and empower ourselves through a fierce and ultra personal struggle for selflessness.

And in so doing, we will entice knowledge and power to the fore. We will step beyond our limits and live life as a *creative* reflection of our own hidden strength. We will affirm ourselves through a life of *rest*, and move one incomprehensible step closer to a *victorious* return to the spirit.

THE CONTRADICTIONS
OF KNOWLEDGE
AND POWER

> *All things come
> to the warrior who rests.*

GOING TO POWER

In don Juan's words, power is a weird affair. It is contradictory by nature and consistently elusive for those who do not already possess it. We cannot simply decide to go to power, because power will never wait where we expect to find it. Power is and power moves. These are the only things that warriors know for sure.

And yet the Toltecs tell us (based on their own experience), that it is possible to go to power. The warriors' dialogue outlines both a passageway and a process of return to the abstract. But by all rational measures, the realization of power's promise seems an impossible task, so what is to prevent us from giving up before we take our first step? There is no simple answer to this question, because in the midst of our confusion lies the essence of *creative victory*.

As insane as it seems, we must begin as seekers by reveling in our contradictions. We must abandon our need to have a rational answer for everything and place our trust in something beyond reason and analysis. The Toltecs tell us that this is the only way we can empower our progress.

It is through the relinquishment of our need for answers that each of us learns to ponder our great fortune and intuit our way along a chosen path with heart. And as we journey on the avenue of power, we find that every turn holds a personal and unique surprise. For there is no reproducible road map to the place where power dwells.

As students of nagualism, we must accept the contradictory premise that the significant transfer of knowledge follows power's agenda and not our own. No matter how much we consciously want to acquire knowledge, the most we can do of our own volition is to struggle to change our emphasis. We cannot change the fact that our ability to go to power exists independent of our waking desire to accomplish this miraculous feat.

THE NOT-DOING OF THE QUEST

Those of us in search of *power's promise* begin with a radical contradiction. We empower ourselves as seekers by not focusing on the overt *doings* of a mechanical search at all. We release ourselves to the *not-doing* of the quest because it is pointless to believe we can pursue a conditional search for the unconditional.

The attitude of people who consciously apply themselves to the process of going to knowledge is not energetically compatible with the indescribable process required to actually rediscover it. Volunteers hold tight to all their conditional assumptions and agendas, and this massive baggage only pins them down in the world that they have already come to know so well.

As warriors, we progress on our path, not by clinging fast to the things we think we understand, but by releasing our stranglehold on those very same conditions. The *doing* of our search gives way to an effortless *not-*

doing, as we patiently allow for the designs of power to bring us an awareness of silent knowledge.

If we gather ourselves and trust in our hidden resources, we simply awake one day to find that power has led us to that which we have waited to find. True knowledge is always a surprise, a magical gift beyond words or imagination. As warriors, we acquire knowledge in an indescribable way and as it comes to us, we contradict ourselves by relinquishing any idea of controlling its further acquisition.

Instead, we hone our intuitive sensibilities so that something unseen can guide us along our way. We open ourselves to power and allow magic to remove all doubts from our minds. As warriors we go to knowledge in a completely contradictory way. We give ourselves *impeccably* to the *not-doing* of discovering it!

It is staggering to realize that it is the *not-doing* of the path of knowledge that eventually leads us to the promise for which we search. As seekers, we learn firsthand that the more we focus our first attention on the acquisition of unconditional knowledge, the more elusive it becomes. By the same token, the more we relax and allow for *not-doing* to emerge in our lives, the more accessible we become to both knowledge and power.

THE ACQUISITION OF ALL THINGS

As warriors we must learn to master the *not-doing* of our lives, if we are ever to acquire knowledge. It is through *not-doing* that we learn to focus ourselves and the emphasis of our energetic resources in an empowering new way. It can be said that we best nurture ourselves through the power of what we don't *do* (since this creates an empowered new perspective for all we *do*).

This is the contradictory essence of *resting*, the key to the Toltec doorway to *victory* and *freedom*. Once we learn to gather and conserve our energetic resources, an incomprehensible movement begins, a *process of power* that carries us to the threshold of our totality.

As part of this baffling process, the warriors who *rest*, are not surprised to find that eventually all things come to them. They have encountered and vanquished three of their four natural enemies, and everything is theirs for the taking.

But *impeccable* warriors, who have acquired the power to access everything, have also spent a lifetime refocusing themselves away from any selfish attachment to those very same conditions. These empowered individuals no longer have conditional desires, even though they know they could indulge themselves to unimaginable heights if they chose to do so.

The warriors for total *freedom* reject indulgence because they know how stupid such a choice would be. They *see* that refocusing themselves on the agendas of the self would only act to reverse their attainments and drain them of their power. Such indulgent behavior can only lead *impeccable* individuals to their own destruction by plunging them back into boredom and the quagmire of a self-obsessed perspective.

True abstract warriors have no interest in indulging or destroying themselves in this way. They have spent a lifetime nurturing their emerging *equilibrium* and will not forsake their gains for petty self-indulgences.

Warriors are detached and at ease with the power they have acquired. They are free from the ties of the black magicians and maintain a commitment to the only thing that still matters to them, their personal *impeccability*. They are warriors of the third attention, and have reached a point on the path of knowledge, where the acquisition of all things is possible. Yet in spite of this attainment, they have no interest in acquiring anything but *freedom*.

To the average person, this may seem a bizarre contradiction, but to *resting* warriors it is really no contradiction at all. Will is quiet and unnoticeable, and the more warriors connect with will, the more they reflect its gentle and unobtrusive qualities.

Actualized warriors have no selfish interests or conditional agendas. They flow effortlessly with power, using their world sparingly and with tenderness. In keeping with the warriors' way, they touch things with an exquisite finesse, leaving hardly a mark behind them when they are gone.

For *los* nuevos videntes, *victory* does not lie in the mechanical acquisition of all things, because there is no peace or satisfaction in such triumphs. Rather than clinging to thoughts of mastery and attainment, the Toltecs choose to abstract themselves instead.

The new seers have no interest in manipulating others or in acquiring wealth and mechanical control. For them, all things have become equal and unimportant in a world of controlled folly. From this *impeccable* perspective, the potential to acquire anything is an awesome gift of power that true warriors know they will never use.

Part Three
The Warriors'
Impeccability

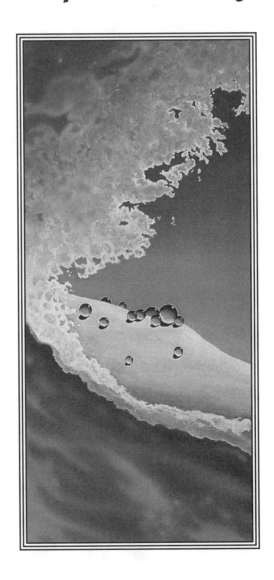

IMPECCABILITY

> *I am the warrior who rests.*
> *I am the warrior impeccable.*

THE WARRIOR IMPECCABLE

By Toltec definition, warriors are people in direct contact with the spirit. This special state of being is contingent upon the ability to establish and maintain a certain level of energy referred to as "personal power." Individuals capable of sustaining this invisible energetic focus eventually empower themselves to step beyond the limits of the tonal.

Impeccability (or *resting*) can be simply defined as the optimum use of our energetic resources. Men and women are said to be *impeccable* when they succeed in rechanneling their energy in the best of all possible ways. For warriors, the methodology of *resting* focuses primarily on the issue of self-importance, which in itself is the most formidable single roadblock to personal empowerment.

In order to become warriors, we must cultivate our own personal brand of *impeccability,* by battling to conserve our energy. The Toltecs tell us that the single most effective way to accomplish this goal is to curtail our own self-importance. They advise us that we must go to war against the part of ourselves that deprives us of our power. They tell us that we must gather ourselves by living the life of the warriors who *rest*.

Resting is a very personal process, and there are as many ways to actualize it as there are human beings on the earth. No prescribed formula for *resting* exists, because *impeccability* is a totally personal state of being. The way we *rest* as individuals depends on the intricacies of our fate and the way those intricacies find expression in the mysterious world of power.

Impeccability is an elusive concept because its realization varies for each and every one of us. No one else can tell us how to *rest*, that is something we must determine for ourselves. For only we can ever truly know the ways that self-importance enervates our personal lives, and only we can actualize a battle plan that will successfully curtail its debilitating effects.

WAR FOR THE WARRIOR

It is the quest for *impeccability* above all things that sends Toltec warriors to war. But the battle that ensues is not a typical conditional conflict. It does not involve armies, or battlefields, or implements of destruction. The warrior's war has only one purpose, the attainment of a state of personal empowerment through the re-prioritization of the items on the island of the tonal.

The Toltec path of knowledge sends us to war, not because we have something to defend, but because we intend with all our might to shatter the mirror of our own self-reflection. We battle, not against some outside enemy, but against the monster of our own self-importance. We struggle, not to overpower others, but to empower ourselves through a transformation of personal emphasis.

War is the natural state for the warrior, not because warriors seek conflict, but because our self-reflective foe has nearly inexhaustible strength. Don Juan alludes to the power and complexity of self-importance when he describes it as a terrible monster with three thousand heads. Whenever we succeed in lopping off one head, thousands of others still remain to hiss back at us. Defeating such a overwhelming opponent requires tenacity and fortitude of the highest order.

The warriors' war is a personal and inner struggle, a silent conflict waged over an invisible resource. Ours is a war that is never completely won, a battle that plays itself out moment by moment in the choices that we make throughout each day.

As seekers we clearly understand what it is we are fighting for. We are not battling for supremacy or mechanical control over others, because our battle plan involves no one but ourselves. We are not waging war for any glory or reward, because our only goal is the realization of our totality. We remain at war, not because we want to, but because it is the only way for us to accomplish our personal transformation. And when all is said and done, we battle for only one reason, because *impeccability* is the only thing that matters on the warriors' path to *freedom.*

THE WAY OF THE IMPECCABLE ACTION

As warriors, we know we will need all our available energy in order to face the unknown and realize our full potential. Shifting our personal emphasis through the actions of an *impeccable* life is one of the primary ways for us to store our personal power instead of squandering it. In this sense, *resting* is of critical importance to every warrior, because unless we become *impeccable,* we remain unable to conserve the energy we need to detach our awareness from the position of self-reflection.

Impeccability is so closely tied to the essence of warriorship that the "warrior's way" is also referred to by the Toltecs as the "way of the *impeccable* action," or the "warriors' road to power." All we require for our journey of return is an appropriate state of *impeccability,* an energetic reality that begins with a single and deliberate act of war.

Power may lead us to momentarily confront self-importance in this way, but the true challenge of warriorship is turning that fleeting assertion into a lifetime of *impeccable* practice. This is a task of awesome proportions, and warriors have nothing to support their efforts except their our own unbending intent to persevere.

To *rest* and be *impeccable* for a lifetime requires a massive shift of our personal emphasis. In a very real sense accomplishing this shift means completely revamping our way of being by altering our most basic reactions to being alive. Instead of senselessly wasting our power on the agendas of the self, we must choose to rechannel our energy in a much more nurturing manner.

Being *impeccable* also means that we are willing to put our lives on the line in order to back up our decisions. As warriors, we must be relentless in our struggle to do consistently more than our best to actualize our choices, whatever they may be. We must also remain intent on empowering our decisions by not second-guessing them once they are made. We must put doubt and recriminations aside as we constantly re-confront our own idiocy and push beyond our limits all the time.

Impeccability is a practicing art form, a state of being that provides for the optimum use of our luminous energy. As a way of life, *impeccability* calls for kindness, wisdom, and an appreciation of beauty. It requires sobriety, frugality, simplicity, innocence, and thoughtfulness. And most of all, it demands a lack of self reflection, a comprehensive detachment from self-pity and the self-important monster that it spawns.

But as much effort as it requires, warriors understand that *impeccability* is not an investment. We cannot see it or touch it. We cannot handle it or trade it like a commodity. *Impeccability* produces no tangible reward, nor can it be threatened once acquired. *Impeccability* is a daily realization, a state of quiet empowerment that warriors renew from moment to moment through the power of their unbending intent.

For the members of the community of warriors, the way of the *impeccable* action is simply the most suitable way to live. The warriors' way sustains us and rejuvenates us and brings us *joy. Impeccability* carries with it its own compensation, because it propels us forward on our impossible journey of return to *power's promise.*

EMPOWERMENT

> *I am the warrior who rests.*
> *I am the warrior empowered.*

THE AVENUES OF POWER

Warriors know that power provides individual avenues of return for every human being on Earth. These avenues unfold before us in accordance with our *impeccability,* and often present themselves in conjunction with our chosen path with heart. But the fact that we are provided with these special avenues does not necessarily mean that we will choose to travel them in the course of our lives.

In fact, it is sad to realize that most people turn a blind eye to their own empowering path. In their ignorance and stupidity, they simply overlook it. They have become disconnected from the spirit, and that disconnection keeps them trapped in a sterile world of their own making.

But as warriors, we are different by definition. We are in direct contact with the spirit, and struggle to make ourselves available to the avenues that intent provides. We battle fiercely in order to store our precious energetic resources, so that the momentum of our efforts might carry us forward on the incomprehensible path to knowledge and *freedom.*

And yet there is nothing we can know about the details of our empowerment. We never cultivate a sense of ownership about the power we acquire, nor do we attach our egos to the magical act of its acquisition. Gathering energy is a humbling affair, it is not an excuse for feelings of egotism, mastery, or superiority. Warriors respect the incomprehensibility of the spirit, and over time, simply experience the fact that traveling the avenue of power is an energizing affair. Power is and power moves; these are the only things that any of us can know for sure.

THE WARRIORS' RESPONSIBILITY

The Toltecs define a person's individual energy level in terms of what they call "personal power." This invisible energetic resource has the peculiarity of being unnoticeable, even when it is being stored, and we are left to gather it as our own personal finding.

As warriors we are concerned about every ounce of personal power available to us, and we learn to conserve it in the most strategic way possible. We know that our journey of return depends entirely upon the energy we are able to store, so we act to plug our points of energy drainage in whatever ways we can.

The warriors *impeccable* are the warriors empowered, because when we learn to curtail self-importance, we energize ourselves by accessing an infinite set of new personal possibilities. As is always the case with the *doings* and *not-doings* of the warrior, personal power is the only thing that matters in the quest to realize our hidden potential.

The Toltecs have shown us that we are no more than the sum of our personal power. It is essential for us to realize that empowerment is a matter of individual choice, and that we alone are responsible for the energetic resources that determine how we live and die. Power offers the same opportunities to each and every one of us, but it is we who decide whether or not to accept the responsibility for those ephemeral gifts.

For the *promise of power* is made to all men and women as luminous beings. No matter how blessed or cursed our lives may seem, this miraculous abstract covenant always remains the same. The fulfillment of *power's promise* involves a lifetime's pilgrimage down the avenue of power, a journey of unimaginable proportions and consequences that few of us are willing to undertake.

Traveling that magical road confronts us with a tangled mass of contradictions. It requires that we maintain an unwavering sense of trust in something totally unseen while accepting the conditional responsibility to wage an outlandish war with our individual sense of self.

Power leads each of us to the threshold of this exquisite and outrageous opportunity at least once in the course of every lifetime. Poised at the portal of intent, each of us is faced with an awesome challenge. Something is shining for us out there, but we hesitate because in order to reach out to it, we must turn our backs on so much that is comfortable and familiar in our lives.

There we stand, teetering on the brink, compelled without reason to believe in our chance to have a chance. We have intuited the existence of something far beyond description, and in a quiet moment of transcendental release, we have clearly recognized the beacon of *power's promise.*

But simply intuiting the possibility of a return to the abstract is not enough to carry us forward. Having caught a glimpse of *power's promise*, we must now actualize theoretical nagualism into a life of practicing warriorship and sorcery. Shouldering responsibility for such an undertaking requires that we focus our intent on the comprehensive reordering of our personal emphasis, because as warriors, we cannot empower ourselves until we decide to become accountable for the energetic condition of our lives.

THE WARRIOR EMPOWERED

D on Juan tells us that *impeccability*, in and of itself, is sufficient to lead us to our full potential. In fact, it is possible for us to empower ourselves without anyone else to guide us. All that we require is a minimal chance to become aware of *power's promise* and the courage to become energetically accountable.

As empowered warriors, we are fully responsible for ourselves. We do not have time to whine and complain about the conditions of our fate. Instead, we gladly accept the hand that power has dealt to us. Being *impeccable* is the only true act of the warriors' empowerment, the only act that is free in the world of intent. The freedom of warriors is to either act *impeccably* or act like idiots, because we know that *resting* alone replenishes us while everything else acts to drain our energy.

Standing on the threshold of the avenue of power, some of us will choose *impeccability* and the life of the warriors who *rest*. We will free ourselves from our conditional limits by becoming accountable for our energetic resources. We will chose actualization over idiocy and invigoration over debilitation, knowing full well that *resting* is the empowering key to our unlimited potential.

PROACTIVITY

> *I am the warrior who rests.*
> *I am the warrior proactive.*

DISENGAGING THE VICTIM

Life in the first attention trains us to be victims. Our own self-pity depletes us and positions us to feel helpless in a world of random outside circumstance. We believe that we are destined to go through life reacting to one conditional circumstance after another.

Average individuals cope with this oppressive perspective by summoning the belief that if they try hard enough, eventually they may achieve some degree of conditional control over life's circumstances. They hope that sooner or later their situations will be explained away or changed or judged through their actions and the actions of other human beings. This erroneous assumption is the last bastion of the powerless victim, the reactive perspective that most people maintain throughout their lives.

Warriors know it is foolish to believe that we can ever wrestle the mechanical conditions of life to the ground. To place our faith in the conditional perspective of the first attention is to keep ourselves separated from an awareness of the truth. The idea that human beings can alter the unbending forces of the universe is arrogant, stupid, and downright disastrous. Power, itself, has shown us that as long as we count on maintaining conditional control of our world, we effectively ignore the existence and the movement of the unalterable essence of the universe.

As warriors, we are in touch with the spirit, and as such, it is impossible for us to ignore its presence. Instead of discarding everything that does not conform to our self-reflective expectations of the world, we accept the unconditional nature of the mystery around us and release our feelings of dependence on conditional control. In the words of the warriors' formula, we are free because *we are already given to the power that rules our fate, and we cling to nothing so that we will have nothing to defend.*

This simple shift of emphasis, this subtle change in perspective, is the key to disengaging the victim within us all. It is also the key to the activation of a new and proactive relationship with power. As warriors we understand that disengaging the victim simply means prioritizing the energetic essence of the unalterable universe over the familiar conditions of the world of solid objects.

Most of us remain victims all our lives because we are simply too short-sighted to do otherwise. Human beings totally commit themselves to the unshakable reality of their description of the world, believing that nothing else can possibly exist beyond it. They exalt the completeness of their world by worshipping it with every drop of energy they have, and struggling to force its random complexities to conform to some logical system or scientific rationale.

But warriors know that the first attention reflections of power will never conform to any rational construct. No matter how hard we try, the essence of understanding remains independent of reason altogether.

There is no point in playing a game of conditional control, because power and its unfathomable designs always holds the trump card.

The sorcerers of antiquity, who destroyed themselves through power objects, have shown us that some unanticipated condition always waits to overwhelm even the mightiest players of such a futile game. The lesson we can learn from them is that controlling anything in the world of solid objects is an illusion.

As warriors, we understand the position of the victim in terms of this pointless struggle for conditional control, and are intent upon empowering ourselves beyond the boundaries of this senseless and destructive cycle. Further more, we have learned that transcending our victimization can only begin when we learn to live another of the warriors' contradictions.

The Toltecs insist that the only way to truly disengage the victim within is to flow with power while accepting responsibility for the circumstances of our lives. Even though we understand on one level that we are helpless creatures surrounded by inexplicable forces, we also know without a doubt that nobody is really doing anything to anybody, much less to a warrior.

Don Juan tells us that the concept of being at the mercy of the wind is simply inadmissible. Warriorship equips us to survive in the best of all possible fashions by exercising an unfathomable "control without control." Instead of remaining reactive objects in a conditional world of first attention circumstance, we transform ourselves into proactive beings flowing freely in a mysterious world of power.

LEARNING TO ACT

The key to disengaging the victim within us is a simple shift of emphasis, an empowering re-prioritization that hinges on our ability to live like warriors. Don Juan tells us that we must learn to act for the spirit alone; to act "just for the hell of it," without expecting anything in return. As warriors we deliberately detach ourselves from the things we *do*, knowing full well that our actions are equal and unimportant in the unalterable eyes of power.

Warriors simply act. Instead of thinking too much about acting or the endless possible consequences of our actions, we choose to proceed decisively in accordance with our intuition and our *impeccability*. We know that if we think about our actions, we will have no choice but to believe that they are important. It is this self-reflective trap that we must struggle ceaselessly to avoid.

As warriors, we empower our actions by not over-analyzing everything we do. We stop second guessing ourselves after we have acted, and most importantly we stop believing that the conditional consequences of our actions are more important than our *impeccability!*

Choosing to act without post-facto analysis and self-criticism empowers us to become proactive in the largest possible sense. We move effortlessly through the complexities of life because we have disengaged ourselves from the self-reflective patterns that define the energy-depleted existence of average individuals.

As warriors, we *see* the world clearly and act with the benefit of our complete *creative attention*. There is no room for self-pity, doubt, or remorse as part of this decisive process. Warriors simply act and then prepare themselves to act again, for this is the way of the *impeccable* action.

THE WARRIOR PROACTIVE

The warriors empowered are the warriors proactive, flowing with power through the actions of an *impeccable* life. We have exchanged first attention reactivity for second attention proactivity. We have learned to move with the world of power instead of constantly reacting to the superficial reflections of the spirit's unfathomable designs.

As warriors, we will not allow the circumstances of the tonal to drain our power and rule our lives. Neither will we remain victims of conditional circumstance and our own self-image. Instead we move with the spirit by maintaining a proactive perspective on every single action that we take. It is this empowered stance that helps us cut through the mire of our inventory while keeping us detached from the debilitating effects of our own self-importance.

As warriors we are never at the mercy of the wind. Don Juan tells us that no one can make us act against ourselves or our own better judgment. The way of the *impeccable* action has tuned us to survive, and we survive in the best of all possible fashions, as power itself directs. As the warriors who *rest*, we calculate our actions and when those calculations are over, we release the outcome into the hands of power. This is the warrior's way of being in control without controlling anything.

Observed from without, warriors live life with a quiet and proactive sense of command. We flow with power while assuming responsibility for the reordering of our emphasis. As warriors we shape our lives, not by struggling with the reactive circumstances of the daily world, but by flowing proactively with the simple awareness of what it means to be alive.

Part Four
The Warriors' Power to Love

PROTECTION

THE WARRIORS' SHIELDS

As the warriors who *rest*, we gather our energy and empower ourselves by virtue of our emerging *impeccability*. This gathering process has many magical consequences, none of which are comprehensible to the mind. One of the most incredulous of these developments is the way in which *impeccable* warriors begin to beckon and confront the nagual.

Most men and women shield themselves from the unknown with the magnitude of their own ignorance and stupidity. They do not recognize the unseen because they simply refuse to allow for the possibility of its existence. The nagual swirls around them every day, but the eyes of average people remain blind to the bitter end.

As warriors, we are no longer average men and women. We deliberately confront our stupidity by struggling to understand our ignorance and our blindness. Power has recruited us as soldiers of the third attention, and *impeccability* has opened whole new worlds before our eyes. But living the tight life of the warrior also has unseen consequences. In addition to enabling us to expand our awareness, it also makes us vulnerable to the assaults of the nagual (which can be deadly if we are not adequately prepared to meet them).

We cannot venture far down the avenue of power without realizing another of the warriors' contradictions. Odd as it may seem, we must soon take steps to protect ourselves from the very power that we seek, because once we embark on the path of knowledge, we open ourselves to forces that can easily overwhelm us. The sorcerers of antiquity have shown us that to confront the nagual without adequate preparation is to flirt with our own destruction.

In order to protect ourselves from the onslaughts of the unknown, we must gradually exchange our old shields of stupidity and ignorance for the new shields of the warriors who *rest.* These new shields are the items that we deliberately select to make our world, the things that will help protect us from the forces that we are trying to use.

The warriors' shields are the elements of the warriors' tonal, the components of a personal path with heart. As we travel the avenue to power, these conditional aspects of our lives give us great pleasure and distract us from our fear. But even more importantly, these new shields help us close our gaps and re-solidify ourselves after direct confrontations with the overpowering nagual.

PROTECTING THE TONAL

The warrior's war with self-importance is really nothing more than a battle to curtail the sterile insistence of the tonal to have everything under its control. Self-importance and indulging die hard, and warriors understand that if they are going to survive, the tonal must be convinced to calmly relinquish its self-reflective insistence on maintaining complete dominion over everything.

Easing control away from the first attention is very tricky business, because the tonal is extremely irascible with regard to its feelings of supremacy. In fact, if the tonal senses that it is losing control, it literally becomes suicidal, preferring to perish in a wave of self-indulgence than to relinquish its authority.

Transforming the facade is difficult, because we must free the tonal from the things that plunge it into boredom and an endless state of self-reflection, while simultaneously protecting its integrity at all costs. As warriors we must remove the crown of emphasis from the tonal with a firm and gentle hand, but once deposed we must also ensure that the tonal is allowed to remain as the healthy and protected overseer of an essential aspect of our awareness.

We accomplish this delicate feat by blending talking and action within a unique self-nurturing context. Warriors understand that the tonal must be convinced with words while the nagual is convinced with actions. By combining some of each in a new and harmonious mix, we accomplish our goal while allowing the members of the one true pair to support and complement each in a way that ensures our ultimate survival.

THE WARRIORS' INACCESSIBILITY

In addition to protecting the tonal from the inevitable onslaughts of the unknown, we also learn as warriors to protect ourselves from the hazards of the first attention world around us. We afford ourselves this protection simply by becoming unavailable to what we wish to avoid.

Warriors are not stupid, we do not stand in the middle of the road. Instead, we act to create a fog around ourselves, a fog that protects us from the limiting thoughts and ties of the black magicians. Warriors are no longer reactive objects available to the buffeting of the world. We have learned to be proactive, and inaccessible by making sure that we cannot be taken for granted or pinned down by the first attention world around us.

But inaccessibility does not imply that warriors are secretive or insidious. Inaccessibility only serves us as a method of *impeccable* protection, not as a ploy to avoid our personal responsibilities. Whatever we do to "create a fog around ourselves" is not the product of some conditional agenda. The impetus for our warriors' inaccessibility flows to us directly from the unalterable abstract.

NURTURING

> **I am the warrior who rests.**
> **I have learned to nurture myself.**

NURTURING THE SELF'S BEST INTERESTS

Before beginning on the path of knowledge, every warrior must confront a series of vital questions. What are the true best interests of my total being and how can they best be nurtured? Is it appropriate to give the self I know free reign over my awareness, or should I redirect my emphasis in keeping with the interests of an unknown self that remains hidden from my first attention?

Warriors always answer these questions in the same way, because as soon as we declare war against self-importance and self-pity, we have already chosen sides. In the moment of our decision to become warriors, we elect to nurture aspects of an unknown self by curtailing the debilitating emphasis of the self we know.

This shift away from self-importance is the Toltecs' method of nurturing the total self's best interests. Even though the average person does not equate the quest for selflessness with personal empowerment, no warrior can deny that this unlikely form of nurturing is the key to the realization of *power's promise*.

ALLOWING FOR MAGIC

D on Juan defines magic as the abstract essence of the world and the force that fills the warrior. Magic is an incomprehensibility that beats at the heart of the warrior's quest, because without it there can be no elation, no lesson, and no realization.

Warriors have learned to allow for magic because there is no viable alternative. Magic is the essence of everything warriors are, everything warriors do, and everything warriors hope to attain. And yet magic cannot be consciously acquired. The only way to access magic is to allow for it to enter our lives on its own terms, and this is a process for which we have no cognitive account.

Allowing for magic is the way we open ourselves to the miracle of *power's promise,* because its the only way for us to reconnect with that which we cannot comprehend. There is no conscious way for any of us to re-acquire the unknown part of ourselves. All we can do is open ourselves to its existence and wait for it to reappear.

By definition, the unknown aspect of the self that warriors seek to nourish exists beyond the limits of thinking or talking or planning or strategizing. Since magic cannot be accessed through traditional avenues, warriors release themselves to an acquisition process that cannot be explained.

Allowing for magic is the *not-doing* of nurturing the total self's best interests. It is an essential skill that all warriors must acquire if they are to begin to unravel the empirical secrets of the assemblage point.

CARING AND NURTURING

Sometimes warriors are lucky enough for power to present them with a special kind of opportunity to nurture themselves. This magical windfall materializes as the chance to care for another human being. As warriors, we consider it an honor to be given such an opportunity, because it allows us to harness our selfishness by extending it to include another.

Caring for someone else a very effective way to shift our emphasis away from the compulsions of our individual sense of self. Any time we can commit to selflessly caring for another, we provide ourselves with an empowering opportunity to give freely and *impeccably* in spite of our feelings. This is an indescribable gift that warriors always recognize and appreciate.

From this perspective, caring can be perceived as a unique form of self-nurturing that has the potential to assist us on the ephemeral path to *victory*. Through a hard-won shift in emphasis and an allowance for magic in our lives, we learn to nurture ourselves by embracing all of our most empowering possibilities.

The bird of *freedom* has given us a glimpse of the promise of those possibilities, and we will not be deterred. We have learned to move with the incomprehensible designs of the spirit, by redefining the scope of our true best interests.

LOVE

THE WARRIORS' LOVE

The average man and woman relate to love from the self-reflective perspective of the tonal. Love, for them, is a romantic ideal that validates their egos and inflates their false sense of self-worth. This familiar form of love is a truly despotic love, because self-pity, self-importance and self-compassion rule its tyrannical domain. As warriors, we are well-acquainted with these temperamental despots of the first attention, recognizing them as the faces of the self that we are battling to curtail.

Those of us on the road to power realize that a debilitating love has no place as part of an empowered life. As warriors, we have declared war on self-importance, and our *impeccability* will not allow us to indulge in feelings that will only rob us of our power.

The warriors' power to *love* differentiates itself from the love of the average person because it does not originate from a self-centered viewpoint. Quite the contrary, it springs from an empowered detachment from the self. The warriors' timeless and unconditional *love* is selfless and unassuming. It is an affection that transcends self-importance and self-indulging because it is linked to a point of origin where no selfish conditions exist to begin with.

From the standpoint of normal awareness, it is challenging for any human being to understand what the selfless *love* of the warrior really is. It is the theoretical *love* espoused by all major religions, but a *love* that is almost never encountered in the functional world.

Unfortunately, most people are conditioned to define love with the focus of the first attention. This means that they come to love with their egos, their expectations, their demands, and their impatience. They expect love to conform to their petty agendas, and when it doesn't, they rage and feel offended.

As warriors we understand that this petty and self-reflective kind of love only impedes our progress on the path of knowledge by creating more boundaries around the items of our world. So instead of worshipping those boundaries and blindly succumbing to their selfish appeal, we struggle to transcend them by opening ourselves to a *love* of a different kind.

While conditional love is centered on the *doings* of the known self, the warrior's unconditional *love* is born of *impeccability* and the incomprehensibility of *not-doing*. The Toltecs have shown us that the warriors' power to *love* is based on an empowering detachment. As we release the things to which we most desperately want to cling, we discover how to *love* with *joy*, efficiency, and abandon in the face of any odds.

SELFLESS LOVE

As warriors, we redefine *love* through our struggle for true selflessness (a state of being that is antithetical in the realm of the tonal). We cannot explain what selflessness feels like, because it exists beyond the limits of language and rational thought. True selflessness stems from an awareness beyond the thinking self, a perspective that only comes to us through a willingness to allow for magic in our lives.

As warriors, we cultivate the experience of selflessness in the same way as we act to nurture the true best interests of our total selves. In order to proceed, we must step beyond our boundaries in an act of impeccable release, thereby allowing magic to redefine the focus of our existence.

An awareness of selflessness can never come to us through desperate acts of hanging on. Clinging to the boundaries of affection only sentences us to a life of boredom and inevitable victimization. The experience of selfless *love* can only wash over us once we have released the things that our first attention self holds most dear.

THE RETURN TO LOVE
AND THE RETURN TO POWER

U ltimately, the warriors' expression of selfless *love* is an *impeccable* reflection of a gathering of personal power, the manifestation of a clearly activated link with intent. Don Juan tells us that *love* has many meanings for warriors, and each one of them mirrors a different aspect of a living relationship with the abstract.

First of all, *love* for the warrior is the unconditional appreciation for the miracle of our own existence, our respect for power, and the way it is reflected in the magic of our ability to be aware. On the avenue of power we learn to *love* every indescribable aspect of ourselves and appreciate the true mystery and incomprehensibility of our luminous totality.

This special brand of selfless *love* is not another form of self-obsession. On the contrary, this *love* functions independently of any selfish agenda, and acts as a magical bridge between the great contradictions of the warrior's world. It is the warriors' *love* that enables us to reach for *power's promise,* because it empowers us to forgive ourselves and *see* beyond our cynical and self-destructive tendencies.

Love for the warrior is also the unconditional affection that we cultivate for this marvelous earth, an entity that we know as a sentient being alive to its last recesses. This gentle, nurturing being soothes and cures us, teaching us *freedom* and liberating our spirit in a way the average individual cannot comprehend.

As warriors, we spend years struggling to create a selfless and unconditional emphasis for our lives, a perspective that will allow for magic to overtake us. The warrior's power to *love* flows from this magical act of release, an incomprehensible act of *not-doing* that launches us far beyond the limits of the known and returns us to an awareness beyond description.

In the final analysis, every aspect of the warriors' *love* is an expression of personal power. *Impeccable* and empowered, proactive and nurturing, it taps the limitless wellspring of our deepest hidden resources.

From the Toltec perspective, it can be said that we go to war in order to accomplish an empowering return to selfless and unconditional *love.* After all, the realization of *power's promise* is no more than a reunion with all that is indescribable about the spirit. Therefore, the return to *love* is the return to power for every single warrior who *rests.*

Part Five
The Warriors' Creative Attention

BREATHING DEEPLY

> *I am the warrior who rests.*
> *I am the warrior who breathes deeply.*

THE MAGIC OF THE BREATH

B reathing is a magical life-giving function. It sustains us on both the biological and energetic levels in ways that are impossible to fully understand. Even so, most people believe they know the importance of the breath. Knowledge of basic biology tells them that breathing energizes the body with oxygen while cleansing it of excess carbon dioxide.

Human beings are always ready to reduce the functioning of the mechanical world to a manageable nonsense. The scientist has degraded the act of breathing to a superficial study in bio-mechanics and the exchange of blood-dissolved gases. The Toltecs, on the other hand, *see* things differently.

They have shown us that breathing also possesses magical energetic properties, that is a vehicle for our luminous energy, invigorating and cleansing the energy body in a way that parallels the functioning of the physical breathing process. As warriors we relate to breathing as more than just an anatomical imperative. We are concerned with the magic of the breath, with its indescribable energetic properties and how they can be applied to empower us on the way to *power's promise.* Breathing for warriors is more than an exchange of oxygen and carbon dioxide, breathing for warriors is an incomprehensible act of power.

THE RECAPITULATION

The recapitulation is one of the most important *doings* of the warrior. Recapitulating is a miraculous act of renewal, an energizing process that cleanses and empowers the warrior in conjunction with the mystery of breathing. The recapitulation is a consummate act of *stalking.* By employing the stalkers' breath, we are able to create a surrogate awareness that makes it possible for us to dart past the Eagle to total *freedom.*

The warriors' recapitulation consists of recollecting every aspect of our life in the greatest possible detail. It is a process that never ends, no matter how *impeccably* it has been accomplished. By recapitulating our lives, we achieve two things. We release ourselves from the energetic ties of others while retrieving energy that we have lost throughout our lifetimes.

The recapitulation is of critical importance to warriors because it is the most expedient way to lose what the Toltecs call "the human form." Don Juan tells us that the human form is a force without form that makes us into what we are as human beings. It is the compelling force of alignment of the Eagle's emanations lit by the glow of awareness in the precise spot where the assemblage point is normally fixated.

Clinging to the human form is singularly responsible for the self-centered thoughts and actions of mankind. As warriors, we are critically aware of this, and as an outgrowth of our struggle for selflessness, we endeavor to lose our affiliation with the force that continually pulls us back into a conditional position of emphatic self-reflection.

Selflessness and formlessness are what we seek, knowing that we must lose our affiliations with both the individual self and the human form if we are ever to return to *power's promise.* Warriorship demands this price of anyone seeking *freedom,* so as we *rest,* we endeavor to recapitulate our lives.

CLEANSING AND RETRIEVING OURSELVES

Warriors intent on a journey of return must learn to cleanse and retrieve themselves energetically. This is the way it must be, because there is no additional energy for us anywhere in the universe. Personal empowerment depends on one thing and one thing only, our individual capacity to conserve the energetic resources that we already have.

The technique of the stalker's breath is a highly effective tool for gathering the finite energy that is our birthright. The specialized breathing associated with the recapitulation is, among other things, an energetic cleansing and retrieval procedure. The exhalation of the breath ejects foreign energy filaments that the body has picked up over time, while the inhalation pulls back energy fibers that have been left behind as part of our personal interaction with others.

As warriors, we know it is imperative to purge and retrieve these luminous filaments in order to effectively gather ourselves. Not only do they have a profound bearing on the level of our personal power, but they are also the energetic basis for our nearly limitless capacity for personal self-importance.

A thorough recapitulation always results in a significant increase in energy. It is a truly empowering *doing*, that produces unimaginable personal consequences. Like breathing itself, the recapitulation is an act of power, an incomprehensible form of energetic release and personal renewal.

The *promise of power* is made to the warriors who *rest* and recapitulate, because the stalker's breath is a lifeline to the abstract. Each enabling breath we take cleanses and retrieves us as we reinforce a new emphasis for our awareness. The longer we remain on the path of knowledge, the more we solidify this empowered outlook, a viewpoint characterized by the actualization of defenseless protection, selfless nurturing, and unconditional *love*.

SEEING CLEARLY

> *I am the warrior who rests.*
> *I am the warrior who sees clearly.*

ASSUMPTIONS AND LIMITS

As warriors, one of the first things we encounter on the road to knowledge is an emerging sense of clarity, a feeling that we are beginning to understand the meaning of life and warriorship. This clarity is a natural by-product of *impeccability*, and a powerful reflection of the shift in our personal emphasis.

We are stunned one day to realize that we have actually begun to *see* the world more clearly. The enhanced level of our personal power has enabled us to begin to perceive life from a new perspective and to claim knowledge that was previously unavailable to us. As our awareness expands, we grow to comprehend the world from a fresh and empowered viewpoint.

Many of our old habits and attitudes fall by the wayside as part of this newfound clarity. Once the balance of power within us has begun to shift, our new perspective will no longer permit us to look at the world in the way that we once did. As warriors we have no choice but to change our minds about a lot of things, including our perspective on first attention assumptions and expectations.

As warriors it is no longer possible for us to assume and expect things about our lives in the way we once did. Our emerging clarity acts to disconnect our conditional focus on what is "probable" in life, while simultaneously refocusing us on what is "possible" and even "impossible" in the warriors' world of power.

The clearer we become, the more we act without assumptions or expectations of any kind. Instead of arrogantly assuming that we know what we will encounter each day, we accept the fact that we live in a mysterious world full of untold surprises . All any of us can be sure of is that power is and power moves. To consume our energy with pointless expectations only impedes our further progress on the path of knowledge.

Our goal as warriors is to be fluid and free, to transcend the limitations of our assumptions and expectations. In the midst of a world unfolding before us from minute to minute, the most we can do is prepare ourselves to meet any situation, expected or unexpected, with equal ease and efficiency.

As warriors who perceive the world more clearly every day, we willingly accept our fate, whatever it may be, because we can never predict how the intricacies of our fate will change before our eyes. Instead of consuming ourselves with worries about our lot in life, we endeavor to use our emerging clarity with the humbleness of the warrior, so that it will carry us forward toward a more selfless perspective on the challenges of being alive.

LOOKING AND SEEING

The Toltecs tell us that the tonal and the nagual make up the one true pair. As we empower ourselves as warriors, we continuously enhance the perceptual capabilities that allow us to explore both these points on the sorcerers' diagram. We learn to "look" more clearly with the eyes of the tonal while we begin to *see* the energetic realm of the nagual with the perceptual capabilities of our entire bodies.

There is an unimaginable difference between looking and *seeing* that warriors experience firsthand. Looking involves clinging to the description of the world, while *seeing* involves an *impeccable* act of release. Looking is a comprehensible *doing* that allows us to view the tonal in everything, while *seeing* is an indescribable *not-doing* that allows us to view the nagual in everything.

The flaw of average people is that they never get beyond looking. Their focus on the mechanical aspects of the everyday world keep them tunneled in on an endless series of conditional agendas that drain their power. The only opportunities they have the energy left to recognize are those in the material world. The darkness and confinement of that self-reflective tunnel keep them focused on the "expected," while effectively blocking their view of anything magically "unexpected."

For most human beings, the opportunity to abstract themselves remains hidden because perceiving that possibility involves processes diametrically opposed to "looking." Since the *promise of power* cannot be perceived using the mechanical senses of the first attention, then it simply doesn't exist for the average individual.

Power continually provides us all with the opportunity to move from the position of the average man or woman to the position of the warrior. All we need to begin is an awareness of the bird of *freedom* as its shadow inevitably glances across our unsuspecting shoulder. For it is then that looking gives way to *seeing*, as the first attention briefly yields to the perceptions of the second. From that moment on our eyes can never be the same, because the Toltecs have shown us that once the spirit has manifested itself to us, the windows of our perception can open to carry us far beyond anything we can imagine.

CREATIVE ATTENTION

From the moment we are born, we begin to develop and refine the attention of looking, the attention of the tonal. As this first attention solidifies and begins to dominate our awareness, it separates us further and further from the attention we had prior to our physical birth, the attention of *seeing,* the attention of the nagual.

This cycle of separation process is a natural part of the human experience, a process that warriors struggle to transcend by living a life of *impeccable* action. Through the *doing* and *not-doing,* of warriorship and sorcery, our goal is to clear the link with intent and reactivate the *creative attention* that we once possessed.

In order to understand the meaning of *creative attention* as I have used it here, we must first examine the Toltec definition of *creativity,* which is described as an incomprehensible capacity that differs totally from the superb "molding" abilities of the tonal. The Toltecs tell us that the first attention is not capable of "creating" anything, it can only witness, assess, and mold things within the world of solid objects. Although this molding ability is often spectacular in scope and form, it cannot be considered *creativity* in the Toltec sense. Pure *creativity* is something indescribable and unconditional, it flows to us silently and directly from the limitless expanse of the nagual.

One of the goals of warriorship is to expand perception until it includes an empirical awareness of *creativity.* In order to accomplish this we must supplement our attention of the tonal with a reactivated awareness of our attention of the nagual. In other words, we must point ourselves back toward the pure *creativity* of the abstract.

Actualized warriors on the Toltec path of knowledge succeed in developing a hybridized attention, a balanced awareness with an empowering *creative* emphasis. This is *creative attention* as *dreaming* has led me to define it, the comprehensive perspective of warrior-sorcerers who have grown to perceive the world more clearly as both lookers and as *seers.*

The warriors who *rest,* develop and expand perception to include both these types of sensory input. Together they form a platform of attention that becomes the launching pad to *victory* and the realization of *power's promise.*

In the warriors' world of power, this harmony of enhanced perception guides us wherever it is we need to go. It empowers us along our path with heart because now we perceive the world with more than just the eyes of the tonal. As the warriors who see clearly, we are the warriors empowered to look and *see* at our own *impeccable* discretion. We are the warriors of a brave new *creative attention,* an awareness that opens us to the magic of all our opportunities, including those that hover unexpectedly in the recesses of the nagual.

CHOOSING WELL

> *I am the warrior who rests.*
> *I am the warrior who chooses well.*

SEEING ALL THE WAY THROUGH

As the result of an incomprehensible gathering of power, we, the warriors who *rest*, awake one day to realize that we have become the warriors who *see* clearly. We have rallied our energetic resources and empowered ourselves to perceive the world *creatively*. Our new expanded awareness mirrors the platform of an emerging *creative victory*, a tentative *equilibrium* between the conditional and the unconditional, the known and the unknown, the first and the second rings of power, the tonal and the nagual.

The utilization of *creative attention* allows us to perceive the challenges of our world with the vision of both the warrior and the sorcerer. We look and *see* the elements of the world around us, relating to everything from a new and more complete perspective.

As the warriors who *see* clearly, we have become proactive perceivers. Our perceptual dualism has liberated us from the position of the victim and opened us to the direct experience of power. We now *see* all the way through the description of the world, a capability that empowers us to choose well.

THE WARRIORS' CHOICES

L ife in the first attention can be defined as an epic series of choices. Each of us defines and redefines our world from second to second through the countless decisions that we make throughout our lives. We are nothing more than an awareness, a point of assemblage on a luminous cocoon. The only thing that matters beyond that energetic absolute is our ability to empower the movement of our assemblage point.

Each of us is faced with the same stream of choices as we wind our way along the path of life. Which fork in the road will we follow? What will our priorities be? How will we be influenced? What will we use as a guide to direct ourselves? The only difference between warriors and average human beings is that warriors utilize these choices as a way of reordering the vital emphasis of their lives.

Choosing *impeccably* (or choosing well) is the only option for warriors intent on finding *freedom.* Our war with self-importance has helped us shift our critical emphasis, and our *impeccable* new priorities empower us to choose well in the face of power.

For warriors, choosing well means more than selecting appropriately from the mechanical options available in the realm of the first attention. Choosing well for those who *see* clearly is something magical and unconditional; it is the strategic arrangement of an *impeccable* life based on the abstract indications of the spirit.

As incomprehensible as it sounds, choosing well means choosing without really choosing at all. For there are no choices in the world of the tonal, there is only humility in the face of power and the unbending intent of the warriors who would be free.

The Toltecs have shown us, and we have *seen* ourselves, that choices belong to the realm of the nagual. This means that there is no way to control the essence of the selections that we make. The most we can do is release ourselves to the incomprehensibility of it all by letting *impeccability* and the manifestations of the spirit guide us along our path.

EMPOWERING DECISIONS

E very decision ever made follows one of two irreversible courses. It either becomes debilitated by doubts, second thoughts, and recriminations, or it becomes empowered through an act of *impeccable* release. Choices become weak and meaningless only if we allow the concerns of our daily lives to drain away their power. Warriors choose well by *stalking* the power of their choices and claiming that precious energy as their own.

Empowering decisions is an essential *stalking* skill that belongs to the art of the warriors' controlled folly. This bridge between the contradictions of life in the first attention provides warriors with an artistic and sophisticated way of being separated from everything while remaining an integral part of everything. The end result is that warriors can immerse themselves in their daily activities to the full extent that their *impeccability* will allow, and then, when all their work is done, stand back and let the spirit decide the outcome without even a second thought.

The Toltecs tell us that we cannot proceed on the path of knowledge until we learn to back up our decisions with everything we have. As the warriors who *rest*, we empower our choices by assuming full responsibility for them to begin with. Then, when we act, we choose to act decisively as we prepare ourselves immediately to act again.

As warriors we know the potential power of our choices can only be actualized if we focus on them properly through the power of controlled folly. This process enables us to bridge the gap between the folly of men and the finality of the Eagle's dictums by releasing our decisions to the designs of power without ever looking back. We humbly accept the results of what we do without judgment or analysis, because we know it is arrogant to think we know what our actions really mean.

It is up to us to set our lives strategically, never looking back or regretting the decisions we have made. We are the warriors who breathe deeply and *see* clearly, *impeccable* and proactive choosers in the conditional world of normal awareness.

Part Six
The Warriors' Transformation

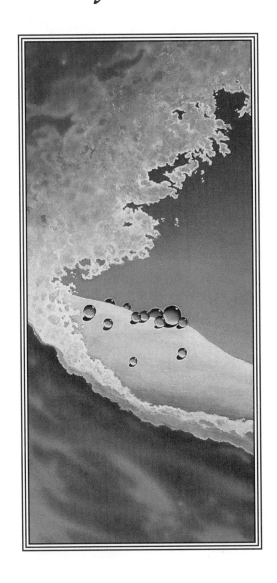

CONSERVING OURSELVES

> **I am the warrior who rests.**
> **I have learned to conserve my own energy.**

OUR MOST PRECIOUS RESOURCE

Seers know that power flows ceaselessly to every sentient being from the moment of birth until the moment of death. The Toltecs have come to call this life-giving aspect of intent the circular force, because when *dreamed*, it gives the feeling of rings. This incomprehensible aspect of the Eagle's emanations is the life-giver and enhancer of awareness. In addition to being the source of our strength, direction, fulfillment, and purpose, it is also the bringer of that which sustains us as luminous beings.

Beyond the circular force, there is no other source of energy for any of us. Realizing this, each of us must come to appreciate the precious energetic resources that flow to us continuously from the Eagle.

But don Juan tells us we must do more than just appreciate this energy, we must assume responsibility for it by going to war with ourselves in a fierce and endless battle for its conservation. We must struggle against the monster of self-importance in order to preserve the precious resource that finds its way to us from the infinite seat of power on a daily basis.

The essence of warriorship is no more than the strategic containment of these energetic resources. We cannot proceed on the path of knowledge without personal power, so we learn how best to gather ourselves through the way of the *impeccable* action.

As warriors we know our enemy, the great robber of power that plagues the human race. But we also know that in the world of the black magicians, this pirate is revered despite his thievery. Self-importance robs people of the power that could set them free, and yet in our ignorance, we still worship this highwayman to the full extent that our meager personal power will permit.

The Toltecs contend that this ignorant and senseless loss of resources is the essence of mankind's plight. In our world gone mad, it is our individual sense of self that rules by virtue of its energetic thievery, and the average human being is just too closed minded to know he has been robbed.

The call to warriorship is the call to rise up against our self-important tyrant. The Toltecs advise us to cast aside our idiocy and stand against the ignorance that once possessed us. They encourage us to demean our own stupidity by supplanting it with a life of *impeccable* action because they have seen that the *promise of power* is made to the warriors who *rest*.

BLEEDING TOGETHER

Warriorship as a way of being demands a tremendous amount of courage. Among other things, it requires unshakable faith in a radical new view of the world. The warrior's way is not for the faint of heart, nor is it for those who are easily swayed by others. Becoming a warrior requires the establishment and maintenance of an intensely personal course, a course that runs counter to the momentum of much of the modern world.

As warriors, we quickly learn that we must turn our backs on the emphatic position of the majority of our fellow human beings. We are living at the height of an age of despair, an age characterized by an excessive concern and emphasis on the individual self. Don Juan tells us that our total involvement with self-reflection is responsible for the homicidal egotism, stupidity, cynicism, and false sense of worth that plagues us as a species.

Self-pity and self-importance are the nemesis of mankind and the source of humanity's endless misery. Warriors know that when human beings create their private hells, those purgatories are not born from evil, they spring instead from a much more insidious and complex source. Our plight is the product of a lack of awareness, a condition born of ignorance, stupidity, and an unwillingness to cultivate an awareness of power as an unalterable absolute.

But as warriors, we insist on confronting mankind's pervasive stupidity with every ounce of determination we can muster. We have caught a glimpse of magic and we will not remain in hell. The spirit has descended on us, and will not permit us to turn back. We have declared ourselves as warriors and now we must stand bravely apart from the self-obsessed reflections of our fellow human beings.

From the moment that power leads us to warriorship, we slowly begin to separate ourselves from the influence of the people that don Juan calls the black magicians (those of our fellow men who would tie us down with their thoughts and conditional agendas). These individuals want us to choose as they have chosen, but as warriors we know that we cannot and must not oblige. The way of the *impeccable* action diverges drastically from the path of the black magicians, because the self that most people worship is the very same self that warriors have sworn to curtail.

Taking a stand that contradicts the consensual views of the prevailing social order is not easy. For most of our lives, we have shared a metaphorical dagger with those around us, the dagger of our collective self-reflection. With this blade we cut ourselves and bleed, senselessly spilling our most precious resources without a thought about the energetic consequences.

The first attention self overrides the effects of this luminous blood-letting by convincing us that we are bleeding together with our fellow human beings in some sort of noble and magnificent act of humanity. This misguided perception could not be further from the truth. In reality, whenever we indulge in opening a vein, we are not sharing anything with anyone. We are simply bleeding away our energetic essence in a pointless and stupid act of self-destruction.

THE IMPECCABLE MECHANIC

As the warriors who *rest*, we have learned to conserve that which is most precious to us. Empowered to *see* clearly, we choose to turn our backs on the senseless energetic bloodletting endorsed by the prevailing social order. As warriors, we respect our energetic resources and will not allow the familiar habits of compulsive self-reflection to drain us of our power.

We are determined to choose for our energetic selves, to choose for *freedom* and the awareness of our total being. And in this *impeccable* choosing, we become conservationists in the largest sense of the word because we have learned to nurture the true ecology of our being.

Warriors know there is no more time for stupidity and the pointless waste of energy! No matter what the black magicians may say and do, we know it is up to us to assume responsibility for the invisible resources necessary to travel the path of knowledge. If we cannot actualize the gathering of our own personal power, then there is not another living soul in the universe that can help us.

The Toltec strategy for energetic empowerment focuses us on a most difficult mechanical challenge. The contradictions of knowledge dictate that in order to nurture the best of ourselves we must remain enmeshed in the worst of ourselves.

As warriors we transcend this staggering challenge by reordering our emphasis and transforming our facade. We sweep clean the island of the tonal and somehow entice power forward in the process. Against all odds we gather ourselves and actualize ourselves as *impeccable* mechanics.

Once actualized in this way, we begin to embody the hard won *victory* of the warriors conserved. We nurture the tonal and keep it strong, but we do not allow its self-destructive tendencies to rule our lives. We take our inventory as the Eagle commands, but we refuse the self-reflective madness of the black magicians. Our controlled folly allows us to hover between our old and new continuities in a way that is incomprehensible even to us. We are the *impeccable* mechanics. We are fully in the world and yet we are not of it.

CONNECTING
OURSELVES

> *I am the warrior who rests.*
> *I have learned to be in touch*
> *with my own strength.*

BANISHING DOUBT

The fallacy of the average individual is a fallacy of awareness. We all have tremendous hidden resources and a living connection to power beyond our wildest imagination, but in our stupidity, most of us choose to ignore the hidden magic of our own existence. Our fallacy is that we turn our backs on the mysterious universe in order to embrace the sterile limitations of our own self-reflection.

Mankind's fatal flaw is that we take ourselves too seriously. We remain glued to the inventory of our reason and will not let it go. We staunchly refuse to deal with ourselves as luminous beings with unlimited potential. Most of us remain victims, plagued by conditional doubts that separate us from the miracle of our true nature.

According to the Toltec perspective, as mankind's individual sense of self developed, the awareness of our link with intent was lost in equal measure. Don Juan tells us that the men and women of today are heir to that terrible disconnection, and therefore the prevailing pattern of life in the first attention effectively separates us from the indescribable source of everything. From this isolated perspective, all the human race can do is express its despair in violent and cynical acts of self-destruction.

As warriors, we struggle to expand our awareness beyond this fatally flawed perspective. The Toltecs have shown us that we were born connected, and that it is only the debilitating effects of our own self-reflection that keep us separated from an awareness of intent. We intuit that magic is our true heritage, and release ourselves to its power by allowing it to get hold of us and banish all traces of doubt from our minds.

THE WARRIORS' CONTROLLED FOLLY

Warriors know that the process of banishing doubt is more a *not-doing* than it is a *doing*. We banish doubt not by consciously eradicating it, but by allowing for the empirical presence of magic in our lives. This allowance for the unalterable involves a miraculous sense of control without control, something that the Toltecs call the art of controlled folly.

Controlled folly is the only way warriors have of dealing with themselves in a state of expanded awareness and perception. It is an art form grounded in a colossal contradiction, a sophisticated way of being detached from everything while remaining an integral part of everything at the same time.

The average person cannot comprehend what controlled folly really is, because like *seeing*, it is something that cannot be accessed through reason. Controlled folly is the application of the seven principles of *stalking* to everything that warriors do, from the most trivial of our daily activities to critical life and death situations.

This performing art of the warrior gives us an unprecedented sense of control without control. Having shifted our emphasis away from the individual self, we feel that we are in command, even though we know we are not controlling anything.

As warriors, we arrange our lives strategically, simply by flowing with power. Through our controlled folly we calculate our actions and then release them into the hands of power the moment we have acted. In this way we remain intimately connected to the world of solid objects while maintaining an *impeccable* detachment all the while.

THE IMPECCABLE INTUITIVE

The Toltecs define intuition as the activation of our connecting link with intent. Warriors intuit a great deal that is unseen in the everyday world, and we use that intuition to accomplish two transcendental feats. One is to conceive the existence of the assemblage point and the other is to make the assemblage point move.

The first of these two attainments is integral to the *preamble of power* while the second defines the essence of the *process of power.* Both accomplishments are vital to the realization of *power's promise,* a transcendental pathway that begins with what can only be intuited.

When power manifests itself to us, our intuition is the only resource capable of recognizing the opportunity at hand. The rest of our thinking sensibilities are at a loss, because they are conditioned to reject the existence of the unknown in the first place. If we as individuals cannot be intuitive to this minimal degree, then our journey of return to *power's promise* ends before it ever has a chance to begin.

For most warriors, summoning the intuition necessary to conceive of their minimal chance is not the problem. It is transforming those intuitive insights into a life of *impeccable* action that presents the real challenge.

In order to accept the Eagle's gift, warriors must follow an intuitive path that embraces a life of energetic conservancy. Therefore, *impeccable* intuitives can be defined as those who have transformed their inherent intuition into a life of practicing warriorship and sorcery! Not only are these individuals in touch with their intuition, they have also succeeded in drawing energy from a conservant lifestyle based on what their intuition has told them.

As *impeccable* intuitives we do more than simply contemplate our intuition, we put our lives on the line by trusting our intuition above all else. Through this courageous process, *power's preamble* evolves into a life of conservancy and empowerment, as the warriors' intuition transmutes itself into the experience of experiences.

It can be said that we begin on the path of knowledge with only our intuition and our intent. The spirit manifests itself to us and an intuitive part of ourselves recognizes the presence of something that is not there. Our physical senses cannot comprehend that with which we are in contact, but our hearts compel us to join the bird of *freedom* just the same. For this is our magical chance to have a chance. This is the outrageous opportunity that power places before us in keeping with the promise always kept. This is our magical window of opportunity, our chance to transform a fleeting intuition into a lifetime of incomprehensible realization.

As practicing warrior-sorcerers in touch with the spirit, we naturally evolve into the embodiment of the *impeccable* intuitive. Our connection with the unalterable is as real to us as our connection to the world of the tonal.

DIRECTING
OURSELVES

> *I am the warrior who rests.*
> *I have learned to direct my life with*
> *my intuition and my intent.*

THE INTERVENTION
OF INTENT

Don Juan tells us we must not worry about procedures because the real direction of our lives is dictated by the intervention of intent. As warriors we must accept the fact that we are in the hands of power, and that learning to direct ourselves is more a matter of flowing with power than it is the conscious establishment of a conditional direction.

In fact, the path of knowledge quickly helps us learn that we direct ourselves best by releasing our notion of mechanical control. As the warriors who *rest,* we act decisively and assume responsibility for the decisions that we make, all the while aware that we are not in control of the conditional world around us.

As warriors, we sensitize ourselves to the whisperings of an intuitive and unconditional guide. We listen for the voice of *victory,* and pay strict attention to the indications of the spirit. In essence, we control our lives without controlling anything. We do our utmost and then, without regrets, we stand back to let the spirit direct the outcome of our actions.

Cultivating our natural intuition is really no more than an act of letting go. We direct ourselves by releasing our expectations and resolving to flow with power in whatever way that power decides to move. Warriors' lives have a miraculous sense of direction, not because we have followed some arbitrary road map of the first attention, but because we have quieted ourselves and realized that the real direction of things is dictated by the intervention of intent.

THE WARRIOR DIRECTED

The totality of awareness has only two primary components, the attention of the tonal and the attention of the nagual. We are all familiar with the attention of the tonal. It is the mechanical part of awareness, the part of ourselves that experiences the self and the everyday world of reason and solid objects. It is the first attention, the first ring of power, the conditional and the known as we are accustomed to perceiving them.

Warriors deal with the attention of the tonal from the perspective of the *impeccable* mechanic. We tune and maintain the tonal as if it were a priceless automobile. We nurture and protect it by truly understanding its working principles. We appreciate its vulnerability, and know that it cannot withstand mistreatment. And ultimately we come to understand the view of the tonal as an invaluable mechanical tool, a precious perspective on which our very lives depend.

Don Juan tells us that as warrior mechanics, we care best for the vehicle of the first attention by reordering its emphatic machinery. We learn to nurture ourselves by rearranging its conditional priorities and implementing a strategy that allows us to conserve our energy. The tonal is mankind's vehicle in this world, it expedites our journey on Earth. As warriors, we go to war in order to care more completely for this priceless vehicle. We sweep it clean and empower it with our *impeccable* capacity for *rest*.

But as important as the vehicle of the first attention is, it is not the ultimate focus of the warrior's way. As *impeccable* mechanics, we have tuned and cared for the attention of the tonal, but not so we might worship it. Our *creative attention* has focused us on the journey of return that we will make in our *impeccable* machine.

In order to realize this ultimate goal, the tonal must have an unwavering sense of direction, an intuitive guidance system that will point it toward the third attention. Like any vehicle, it requires an effective navigator, a force to direct it along the road it was meant to travel.

Establishing a guidance system for the vehicle of the tonal is a vital issue in all warriors' lives. It involves changing our perception at its social base and shifting our emphasis away from the ties of the black magicians. For in order for warriors to best direct themselves, they must learn the art of *creative* navigation.

CREATIVE NAVIGATION

A verage people direct their lives with nothing more than the faculties of the tonal. In other words, they allow their first attention awareness to act as their only directional guide. Warriors recognize this as a very shortsighted approach, because even though the first attention appears to have navigational qualifications, it is sorely limited in both its perspective and its directional capabilities.

The struggle to *see* clearly and choose well has given us a clear perspective on the strengths and weaknesses of the first attention. We know that we must nurture and protect the tonal as the overseer of the mechanical portion of our awareness, but we also know that we must go to war in order to curtail the debilitating aspects of the individual self. It is up to us as warriors to ensure that the first attention is not given free reign as the unquestioned navigator for the vehicle of our journey of return.

As *impeccable* intuitives, we know that we must allow an unseen navigator to guide us back to the abstract. We must entrust our *impeccably* tuned machine to the strength of something totally invisible and incomprehensible, a force that we cannot explain or understand.

Once touched by the manifestations of the spirit, we travel the path of knowledge by allowing ourselves to be guided in a whole new way. We cultivate an abstract directional system beyond the attention of the tonal that allows power itself to direct us on our journey. Miraculously, this release permits the *impeccable* mechanic and the *impeccable* intuitive within us to work side by side toward the realization of a common goal.

As the warriors who *rest*, we navigate through life by abandoning the road map of assumptions and expectations. We are the warriors conserved and the warriors connected, the warriors who entice the spirit forward as the *creative* navigator in our lives.

Directing ourselves to *power's promise* is a process of inconceivable dimensions and must be respected for what it really is. It is a miraculous form of *not-doing;* an incomprehensible feat of *creative* navigation that leads us to the balancing platform of our *victory* of awareness.

Part Seven
The Warriors' Equilibrium

THE JOY
OF BALANCING

> *I am the warrior who rests.*
> *I have balanced sobriety and abandon.*

A RETURN TO JOY

Don Juan makes it clear that *joy* is the ultimate accomplishment of *impeccable* warriors. *Joy* is a condition of our character, it stems from our ability to *rest* and from a full awareness of our efficiency in any conceivable situation. We are joyful because our *love* is unalterable and because we are humbled by our great fortune at having found a challenge. We are joyful because we have willingly accepted our fate and because we act for the spirit alone.

As warriors we *see* the difference between *joy* and the pursuit of self-indulgent gratification. The *joy* of the warrior is not a conditional feeling of the first attention, it is something that flows to us directly from the seat of power. As warriors, we do not go in pursuit of *joy*, we simply allow *joy* to descend upon us as a result of our emerging *equilibrium*. *Joy* comes to the warriors directed, to the warriors who walk their personal paths with heart.

Joy emerges for those of us who succeed in striking an incomprehensible balance between the blatant contradictions of knowledge and power. As joyful warriors, we have learned to harmonize ourselves and the forces around us in order to meet the fundamental challenges of warriorship and sorcery. *Joy* is the *joy* of balancing, an awareness that hovers miraculously between the contradictory forces of sobriety and abandon.

THE BALANCE OF THE WARRIOR

The path of knowledge is paved with contradictory propositions. Striking a balance between these conflicting opposites is the key to launching ourselves beyond the platform of power to our ultimate *creative victory.*

The resolution of power's contradictions requires the utmost of any warrior. We must accept without accepting, and disregard without disregarding. We must act as if nothing has ever happened, and yet accept everything at face value. We must vanquish our reason without abandoning it, and remain patient even though we know we do not have a moment to spare.

An empowering new awareness emerges when we pit the contradictory views of the world against each other and succeed in wriggling between the polarity of those perspectives. This crack between conflicting realities is the warrior's gateway to the truth, a perspective that, by definition, is neither here nor there. Yet despite the logical reasons why this balance should not be possible, warriors thrive in the midst of its impossibility just the same.

This unimaginable state of being is embodied within the life experience of every warrior who *rests.* It is the emerging awareness of an *equilibrium* that cannot be explained or understood.

Recreating the balance of the warrior is part of every human being's birthright, but those on the path of knowledge seek it in particular. For it is this miraculous harmony of opposites that defines the interim realization of the warrior-sorcerers' *creative victory.*

THE MIRACLE OF EQUILIBRIUM

D on Juan tells us that all human beings begin life with a spiritual imbalance of some kind. During the course of our time on Earth it is up to us to identify that imbalance and assume responsibility for equalizing it. In Toltec terms, this means that we must struggle to regain the awareness that we have lost. If we fail, we don't regain our balance before we die.

The balance that warriors seek is embodied in the *equilibrium* of the Toltec path to *freedom,* the contradictory juxtaposition of the components of the one true pair. *Equilibrium* is the harmony of the warriors' sobriety and the sorcerers' abandon, the interim balance of an emerging creative victory.

Sobriety beats at the heart of warriorship, it is a facet of an *impeccable* tonal. Sobriety is the weapon with which we battle our own self-reflection, an empowering state of mind that reflects our profound bent for objective self-examination and understanding. Sobriety is the warriors' quiet internal strength that finds expression in our feeling of being at ease with the world.

But power requires more from warriors than just sobriety. We must also live with intuitive abandon, because that is how we reflect the reality of the unfathomable nagual. As warriors we create gestures for the spirit, by trusting in a power that we cannot see or comprehend. Our sense of abandon expresses itself in our fluidity and our lightness, in our ability to laugh at ourselves and to act soley on the basis of our intuition.

As warriors in balance, we embody a state of being characterized by both sobriety and abandon. This abstract *equilibrium* of the Toltecs is not a conditional concept, it exists independent of the first attention's tendency to pair off the items of our world. For warriors, *equilibrium* is a reflection of the harmony between the components of the one true pair, a delicate balance that mirrors an interim awareness of our totality.

As we wriggle between the contradictions of our world, warriors encounter an anomaly that is staggering and sublime. We return to *equilibrium* to find a transcendental calm in the midst of our never-ending battle with the self. For the Toltecs, this is the ultimate *joy* of warriorship, this is the quintessential *joy* of balancing!

AN APPROPRIATE
DETACHMENT

> *I am the warrior who rests.*
> *I have shattered the mirror*
> *of my own self-reflection.*

THE WARRIORS' RUTHLESSNESS

The eyes of the warriors who *rest* shine with the gleam of ruthlessness and actually succeed in beckoning intent. These statements are beyond the thinking comprehension of the average person, because ruthlessness as the Toltecs define it is a concept beyond language and explanations. Ruthlessness is a state of being that can only be experienced by individuals with sufficient power to reach the place of no pity.

The warriors' ruthlessness is no more than a position of the assemblage point, a level of intent that warriors have attained. It is not harshness or cruelty, nor is it a matter of being cold-hearted or mean-spirited. In fact, by the Toltec definition, ruthlessness has no first attention attachments at all. On the contrary, it is a condition of awareness that reflects an *impeccable* detachment, a state of complete indifference to our own self-pity.

Ruthlessness serves the warrior, not as a strategy for controlling and overcoming others, but as an extension of the *impeccable* quest for selflessness. Ruthlessness is the first principle of sorcery, ruthlessness is the foundation of the warriors' sobriety and the basis of our quiet inner strength.

THE MIRROR OF SELF-REFLECTION

The prevailing social order conditions us to cling to everything. We are inappropriately trained to believe that it is possible to maintain mechanical control of our world, and that we will be all right if we just cling tightly enough to our false sense of command.

Warriors know there is no such thing as conditional security, there is only power moving in a mysterious universe. We also know that committing our allegiance to the position of self-reflection relegates us to the reactive status of the victim.

Nevertheless, as typical members of the human race, each of us is trained to abandon our intuition while desperately clinging to that which we think we know. The everyday world of rational probabilities becomes the benchmark by which we live. We create an ever-refined attention of the tonal until we believe with unshakable certainty that the world of solid objects is all there is.

But as warriors who *see* clearly, we refuse to inhabit such a boring and sterile place. We know that this world of the first attention holds no room for miracles; that its narrow boundaries only define the prison of the self-obsessed.

The attention of the tonal is like a tunnel with mirror-covered walls. The most its confines can do is reflect the endless faces of the individual self. As warriors, we are determined to escape this sterile hall of mirrors. We seal our allegiance to the abstract instead of committing our energetic resources to the self-absorbed obsessions of the first attention.

As the warriors empowered, our intent is to break out of the tunnel of self-reflection, and shatter its mirrored walls with the force of our *impeccability*. By restricting our involvement with our own self-image, we burst beyond our boundaries into the vast expanse of the limitless unknown.

THE WARRIOR DETACHED

As warriors, we spend a lifetime developing an appropriate detachment. This is not a contrived sense of separation or indifference, nor is it an excuse to run away from ourselves or the circumstantial aspects of our lives. The warriors' detachment is born out of conviction. It is a reflection of our *impeccability*, not a product of our laziness and indolence.

In the world of power, each of us must struggle to distance ourselves from the things that deprive us of our energy, the things that keep us victims in the world of solid objects. The warriors who *rest* are the warriors detached, the warriors who know the importance of release.

The Toltecs' example shows us that we must refuse to cling to any condition of our lives save the condition of our own *impeccability*. Through the power of our detachment, we must gently release our stranglehold on everything that binds us to this world. This long list of items includes such things as self-importance, our material and emotional holdings, and our affiliation with the human form.

Don Juan tells us that we must even vanquish reason through our *impeccable* sense of detachment. By this he means that we must suppress the debilitating effects of the first attention, not our capacity for rational thought per se. As warriors we strive to be true thinkers, rather than individuals who simply love the orderly works of reason. As with all other forms of *impeccable* release, when we curtail our compulsive attachment to reason, we allow our awareness of the unalterable to emerge more freely in our lives.

The key to the warriors' detachment is the awareness of death. Only the active force of death is sufficient to ensure that we can neither deny ourselves anything nor cling to anything in this life. With death as our adviser, detachment becomes an empowering affair that promotes the warriors' quest for total *freedom*. By separating ourselves from self-importance and the conditions of our circumstantial world, we are free to flow with power towards the realization of the promise always kept.

THE WARRIORS' EMPHASIS

> *I am the warrior who rests.*
> *I have transformed my own facade.*

THE CORE OF EVERYTHING GOOD,
THE CORE OF EVERYTHING ROTTEN

D on Juan tells us that the first attention is trained to focus doggedly, for that is how each of us maintains the integrity of the world. This familiar aspect of our awareness is pure magic, enabling us to impart order to all that we perceive. The first attention (or the tonal) is the organizer of the world, the sum total of everything that meets the eye and everything the intellect can conceive of.

The tonal is part of the one true pair, and as warriors, we appreciate it as an invaluable component of our total energetic being. The fact is, however, that self-importance belongs to the realm of the tonal, and since we have declared war on this debilitating aspect of ourselves, we know that the tonal is where our battle must ensue.

But in our effort to wage the warriors' war, we encounter a bizarre dilemma. The problem with self-importance is that it lies at the core of everything good and the core of everything rotten within us. Unfortunately, both aspects of self-importance are tangled up with the rest of our waking awareness and it is up to us to somehow curtail the worst about ourselves while preserving what is best about ourselves. Even don Juan tells us that this process requires a masterpiece of strategy and can only be accomplished by warriors with the utmost *impeccability.*

As we rise to meet this challenge, we are clear about two very specific things. First of all, we know that we must battle to curtail self-importance in order to plug our points of energy drainage. But as we wage that internal struggle, we have also learned that we must protect the essential integrity of the tonal at any cost.

Whatever our *doings* or *not-doings* as warriors, we know about the suicidal tendencies of the first attention and how it must be disengaged with great finesse. We may have gone to war with the worst of ourselves, but we will not allow the core of everything good to perish in the fight.

DETHRONING THE DESPOTS

A s the warriors protected, we know we must proceed with extreme caution as we dethrone the despots of the first attention. If we unseat them too forcefully, they are likely to take a suicidal plunge that will threaten our very existence as human beings. Don Juan tells us that warriors do not seek death, and so we must deal gingerly with these despotic aspects of ourselves if we are to ensure the rearrangement of our personal emphasis as well as our own survival.

From the Toltec perspective, the despots of the first attention are not really malicious enemies. The debilitation they cause is more a product of the way the must be function in order to accomplish their miraculous tasks. They behave the way they do simply because their perspective is limited by the boundaries of the world that they so totally and accurately define.

It is unfortunate that the overall scheme of awareness leads these tyrants of the tonal to want to rule us and command our full energetic attention. They have lorded over us for most of our lives and remain convinced that they must maintain complete control of our awareness or die in the attempt.

This suicidal tendency is a powerful indicator that these despots have been left to rule our awareness from a sterile and totally disconnected perspective. In fact, the only reason they become despotic is because they are so short-sighted with regard to the energetic realities of the mysterious universe. The children of our misguided self image are simply not equipped to perceive the scope and true best interests of our luminous reality.

As warriors who *see* clearly, we manage these unruly despots as if they were undisciplined youngsters unwittingly left to run the kingdom of our awareness. Like firm and loving parents, we gently remove them from a position of control, much as we would one of our own children who had gotten out of hand.

We are the warriors who *rest,* and more than anything, we are intent upon maintaining the health and integrity of the entire family of our awareness. Self-importance and egomania are despots to be sure, but in our role as nurturing parents, it is up to us to curtail the emphasis of these despots while keeping the true best interests of our total selves in mind.

Even though we go to war with the tyrannical part of ourselves, we know we must also maintain a perspective of unconditional *love* for all aspects of our awareness, including self-importance. This means that we must act with both forcefulness and finesse as we reorder the critical emphasis of our awareness. To carelessly annihilate any aspect of the tonal is a stupid and senseless act that can only lead to our own self-destruction.

As warriors we avoid this problem by nurturing and parenting ourselves in the best of all possible ways. We dethrone the despots of the first attention by acting decisively and with temperance. We make no bones about removing them as the rulers of our awareness, but once unseated, we maintain these essential aspects of our awareness as loved and necessary overseers of a critical part of our total being.

TRANSFORMING THE FACADE

As warriors, we regain our balance and personal power by putting the house of our energetic awareness in order. Despotic children without perspective are simply not permitted to rule the kingdom. With a firm and loving hand, we remove them from the throne in order to reinstate them more appropriately within the context of our warriors' facade.

The Toltecs define transforming the facade as the sustained act of shifting the place of prominence of key elements on the island of the tonal. We learn to emphasize important things (like *impeccability*) while de-emphasizing the things that drain our power (like self-importance).

This re-prioritization is the essence of the warrior's transformation, which is more a shift of emphasis than a "transformation" per se. Don Juan tells us that there is nothing to change in a luminous being, so as warriors we transform ourselves, not by changing into something new, but by strategically reordering our priorities.

Transforming the facade can be understood as a product of the warriors' empowered parenting skills. We assume responsibility for managing the self-reflective aspects of awareness that squander our most precious resources, and empower ourselves by emphasizing those parts of our totality that reinforce our true best interests. This transformation of emphasis is the ultimate act of nurturing, the responsible and loving way in which we parent our total selves.

Part Eight
The Warriors' Victory

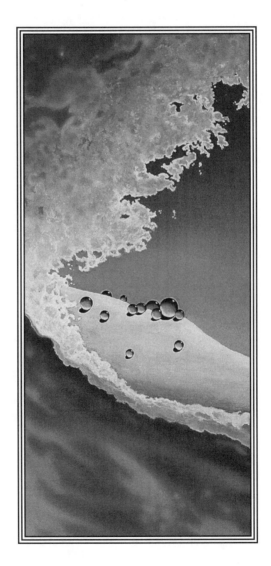

BECOMING
THE FLYER

> *I am the warrior who rests.*
> *I have prepared myself for dreaming.*

THE GATHERING

Resting is an energetic gathering, a magical consolidation of personal power. As the warriors who *rest,* we gather ourselves by learning to live *impeccably,* and as we do, we free our surplus energy for the activation of our dormant second attention.

In the Toltec scheme of things, the gathering is a way of describing the incomprehensible acquisition of personal power. It is a process without rules, predictabilities, or concrete terms, a phenomenon free from scientific laws or logical constraints. The gathering is simply another mysterious reflection of that aspect of the universe that can never be described.

Despite its ephemeral nature, warriors focus on the gathering with an unbending intensity. Nothing matters to them except *impeccability,* and *impeccability* is what the gathering is all about. Warriors summon a fierce concentration in order to consolidate themselves for their journey of return, but rather than concentrating on a typical focus of control, they strive to develop a particular brand of concentration involving an indescribable focus of release.

As with so many other aspects of the Toltec path of knowledge, the gathering emerges from the heart of a contradiction. There is no doubt that we must be focused to be *impeccable,* and yet in order to gather ourselves, we must also de-focus ourselves in equal measure. It is this remarkable combination of sobriety and abandon that enables us to consolidate our energetic resources as part of an exquisite *equilibrium* beyond the reaches of our conscious control.

THE WARRIOR PREPARED

The art of *dreaming* requires energy that most of us do not have, because we have squandered those resources on the agendas of the self. As warriors however, we learn to conserve our personal power and use it for the expansion of our awareness. *Resting* prepares us for *dreaming* simply because it facilitates the accumulation of energy necessary to experience the movement of the assemblage point.

The warriors' way enables us to lay the energetic groundwork for a journey of return to the abstract. And even though we do not know where the avenue of power will lead us, we transform ourselves into the warriors prepared and assured; not because we are cocky and over-confident, but because we have sought *impeccability* in our own eyes and found humility.

The warriors prepared are the warriors who have set up *dreaming* (as the Toltecs define it). By practicing the art of *stalking*, we have reordered the emphasis of our first attention in the most strategic way possible. It is this *impeccable* groundwork that prepares us for the magical art of *dreaming,* the art of focusing our second attention in a nurturing and empowering way.

Don Juan defines *dreaming* as a process of internal awakening, a process of gaining control of the incomprehensible. *Dreaming* is the lucid *not-doing* of warriors, the realization of our unconditional possibilities. *Dreaming* opens the door to other perceivable worlds and prepares the *dreamer* to enter those worlds in full awareness. *Dreaming* is a journey of unthinkable proportions, the gateway to the light and darkness of the universe.

SETTING UP DREAMING

For the warriors who *rest, dreaming* is an inevitable act of power. It manifests itself as a separate reality once we have gathered ourselves sufficiently to become aware of it. Don Juan tells us that the requisite to *dreaming* is the re-deployment of our energy. As warriors we accomplish this rechanneling of resources by transforming our personal emphasis and conserving our personal power. It is this *impeccable* conservation process that the Toltecs call "setting up *dreaming*."

As the warriors who *rest* we are the warriors empowered to take flight on the wings of intent. We have worked tirelessly to build our inner strength, so that when *dreaming* overtakes us, we will have the sobriety necessary to avoid its pitfalls.

The Toltecs describe *dreaming* as the "gateway to infinity" or "the sorcerers' way of saying good-night to the world," but in more pragmatic terms, *dreaming* can simply be described as a practical way of putting dreams to use. In conjunction with the art of *stalking,* the goal of *dreaming* is the controlled movement and fixation of the assemblage point. This process is the key to everything that warrior-sorcerers do, from the *doings* and *not-doings* of their everyday lives to the magical culmination of the transcendental flight to *freedom.*

Literally or metaphorically, becoming the flyer is an incomprehensible feat, an inevitable act of power for the warriors who *rest.* Flying is the actualization of the warriors' ability to hold tight to the lines of the world, as well as the living realization of the abstract flight to *freedom.* Either way, we take wing as a result of the incomprehensible movement of the assemblage point across an indescribable bubble of luminosity.

And so, as the warriors gathered and prepared, we eventually become *impeccable* flyers. And in the incomprehensibility of it all we find the realization of our *dreaming victory,* our reconnection with intent through the magic of a path of dreams. From the human standpoint, we cannot explain the miracle of our flight, we can only soar in breathless wonder and be thankful for our chance to have a chance.

WALKING THE PATH
WITH HEART

> *I am the warrior who rests.*
> *I have joyfully walked*
> *my personal path with heart.*

JOY AS AN INDICATOR

L ife presents each of us with an infinite number of different paths, any of which we can freely choose to walk. Most men and women pay relatively little attention to this critical selection process, but not so the warriors who *rest*. We know the ultimate importance of our path, and so we do our best to breathe deeply, *see* clearly, and choose well.

For most people, selecting a path to walk is a rather superficial and arbitrary process. Criteria for this choice tend to be first attention conditions and nothing else. The avenues that attract us are the paths that require little effort or appear to offer conditional rewards. If a path promises fame or fortune, power or prestige, it is likely that we will choose it without any consideration for a larger perspective.

Choosing a path based on these kinds of evaluations alone is simply not enough for the warriors who *rest*. In order to choose well, we know we must perceive our choices from a more complete perspective, and that our big picture must include more than first just the obvious parameters of the first ring of power. As warriors, we choose with our *creative attention,* an empowered perceptual faculty that transcends the mechanical limits of the tonal.

This enhanced perspective allows us to choose our path from a more heartfelt point of view. We will not ignore the mechanical realities of the various options before us, but neither will we make our selections on the basis of those conditions alone. As warriors we find a road to travel, but we select it with the help of the spirit's unconditional guidance.

Whatever the mechanical consequences, we know we must prioritize the path power points out to us. We must allow our sense of *creative* navigation to take priority over what we expect about the details of our lives.

It is only our *impeccable* intuition that can guide us to a path of empowerment where we can thrive at our magical best. Regardless of how that road may look to our eyes, we must *see* and follow the indications of the spirit just the same. The superficial aspects of our path with heart may conform to our first attention agendas or they may not. Whatever the case, the only thing that matters to us as warriors is choosing a path where *joy* will rise to meet us where we walk.

But as I have described earlier, the *joy* of the Toltec warrior is not the joy of the average person. It is not petty self-gratification or wanton self indulgence. *Joy* is not the realization of selfish or egomaniacal attainments, nor does it spring from the exercise of control over others, a false sense of superiority, or a fake sense of worth.

Joy for the warrior is not a reflection of stupidity! *Joy* is transcendence! It is the soaring of our hearts when we are in touch with the spirit. It is the indescribable feeling of knowing what is right and appropriate at a given moment. It is an intuitive and unconditional elation, a magical feeling of connectedness to power and the inspiration of its universal promise.

In this sense, *joy* is the warriors' indicator, because wherever we find it is where we find our *victory*. *Joy* is a reflection of the nagual, a direct manifestation of the designs of the spirit. *Joy* is a contradiction, at once ephemeral and empirical, indescribable and at the same time real. *Joy* is nothing less than pure magic and it waits for any warrior who will assume the responsibility to discover it.

Joy is an essential navigational tool for the warriors directed. It is an unconditional reflection of *power's promise* and a guidepost for the warriors who *rest*. True *joy* as the warrior defines it is a miracle of the highest order, an unwavering beacon that guides us through the mire of our first attention agendas. *Joy* is the magic that flows to us on our nurturing path with heart.

THE EMPOWERING PATH

With *joy* as our indicator, the selection of an empowering path becomes a natural process. We choose well because we insist that the conditions of the everyday world take a back seat to the voice of *victory*. We select a path in our true best interests by allowing *joy* and intuition to light the way.

Don Juan tells us that there is only joyful traveling on the empowering path with heart. No matter what the road may look like, we know our chosen path will nurture and strengthen us as we travel. As warriors, we find our way to *victory* because we center our waking lives around a path that will uplift us. From an energetic standpoint, warriors understand that to choose in any other way is suicide, and we will not permit the despots of the first attention to coerce us onto a path that can only debilitate and destroy us in the end.

In the final analysis, don Juan tells us that warriors choose a path with heart and follow it. And as we travel we rejoice and laugh and *see* and know. For as long as we walk our chosen path, we will remain as one with it, joyous and empowered on the way to *power's promise.*

THE NAVIGATOR

As warriors on our path with heart, we are warriors on the road to power. We are joyful and directed, and yet incredulous and in awe. We cannot know how we have wriggled between the contradictions of our lives, but we know our mood is joyful just the same. We cannot explain how power has found its way to us, but we know that we have gathered it just the same.

As the warriors who *rest*, we are warriors given to the power that rules our fate. We no longer chart our progress by the expectations and first attention landmarks that guide the lives of others. Ours is a different course, established by an intuitive connection to forces that we cannot understand. We navigate our way to *victory*, not by virtue of our reason and self-reflection, but by releasing ourselves to the unfathomable designs of the spirit.

Power is and power moves; these are the only things that warriors know for sure. As *impeccable* navigators, we respect the designs of the spirit and do not struggle against that which we can never understand. Instead, we move through life by flowing proactively with power's unseen current.

And so, as the warriors gathered and prepared, we eventually become *impeccable* navigators. And in the incomprehensibility of it all we find the realization of our *stalking victory,* our reconnection with intent through the magic of a path with heart. From the human standpoint, we cannot explain the miracle of our travels, we can only walk in breathless wonder and be thankful for our chance to have a chance.

CREATIVE VICTORY

> *I am the warrior who rests.*
> *I have found peace in my creative victory,*
> *a victory without glory or reward.*

VICTORY AND THE RETURN TO CREATIVITY

Victory for the warrior is an emerging realization; it is not the conditional victory of the world we know. *Victory* is not a trophy, or a certificate or an award, it brings with it no glory or reward. *Victory* is not a prize to be displayed, nor fuel for the fires of the first attention despots. As warriors we understand that *victory* is not an excuse for more stupidity! *Victory* is a manifestation of our totality, a reflection of the essential and incomprehensible oneness of the universe!

The warrior's *victory* is quiet, unobtrusive and unalterable. It is a triumph that emerges from a personal and private battlefield; the ascendancy of a loving and nurturing parent over a most unruly child. *Victory* is nothing more than an evolving realization of power and its movements, an awareness of what we truly are and what we always have been.

Victory is an awareness of both components of the one true pair. *Victory* is immutable, it reflects the essence of what is true and unchangeable about everything. *Victory* never stops existing, it is always there before us in its awesome splendor. It is only our awareness of *victory* that falters and becomes disconnected. When we empower and reconnect ourselves, we are *victorious!*

Victory is not a destination, it is the avenue of power. Don Juan describes our journey of return to the abstract, as a *victorious* return to the spirit after having descended into the private hell of the cynical and egomaniacal self.

In Toltec terms, this triumphant return to power can be categorized as a *creative* process because it is a process that flows to us directly from the abstract itself. *Victory* is a process of realization that leads us back to our total selves, back to the true *creativity* of the nagual.

Don Juan defines *creativity* as a direct expression of intent, not something that can be molded or assessed within the conditional limits of the first attention. *Creativity* for warriors is an incomprehensible surfacing of the spirit, an expression of the unalterable that can only be experienced with the sorcerers' awareness.

In this sense, the emerging realization of our totality is always a *creative victory,* because *equilibrium* and *freedom* flow from an indescribable process that moves the assemblage point. Don Juan tells us that the hidden capacity for this ascendant triumph is something shared by every human being alive. The only thing that distinguishes us as warrior-sorcerers is a commitment to a way of life that reactivates the magical promise of that potential.

VICTORY AND DEFEAT

One of the inevitable results of a life of warriorship is an emerging creative attention. We perform *creatively* when we act unconditionally and for the spirit alone. We think *creatively,* when we finally relinquish our stranglehold on reason and the conditional construct of our world. We choose *creatively* when we allow ourselves to navigate with our intuition and our intent. And we exist *creatively* when we commit ourselves to the way of the *impeccable* action and the incomprehensible *not-doings* of our lives.

This *creative* approach to living also allows us to understand that both winning and losing are part of the same controlled folly. In the eyes of those who *see,* there is no difference even between *creative victory* and defeat, because as circumstantial expressions of the tonal, both are equal and unimportant in the unalterable scheme of things.

Don Juan explains that the only one difference between being victorious and being defeated is a variation in levels of personal power. As the warriors who *rest,* we find our way to *victory* because we have gathered our energetic resources. On the other hand, *victory* tends to elude those who have simply allowed their power to drain away.

Despite the obvious superficial implications of this distinction, no warrior can say that being *victorious* is preferential to not finding *victory* in the course of one's life. If the challenges of warriorship and sorcery present themselves as part of our path, then all we can say is, "So be it!" and proceed.

But in the event that our minimal chance doesn't materialize, then the same "So be it!" is still our most appropriate reply. For by the seer's own unalterable criteria, one conditional position cannot be superior to another. After all, the *promise of power* is made to all men and women as luminous beings, whether they follow the bird of *freedom* or remain behind.

THE CREATIVE VICTOR

W arriors know that *creative victory* is an evolution of awareness that unfolds in keeping with power's own design. It is an emerging perception of our totality that brings us ever closer to the realization of *power's promise;* a constantly expanding state of being that reflects itself through the warriors' waking awareness and level of personal power.

Creative victory is a daily affirmation of what is real, but it comes and goes in an instant, leaving no trace of laurels on which to rest. We have no time to relax and pat ourselves on the back, for we know that today's *victory* will not last. In order to keep our minimal chance for *freedom* alive, we will have to battle just as hard tomorrow as we have valiantly fought today. But as we struggle, we will rejoice in our *creative victory* without glory or reward. For no one can convince us that magic does not exist; we have experienced it directly in the ways that only *creative victors* can.

Part Nine
The Warriors'
Potential

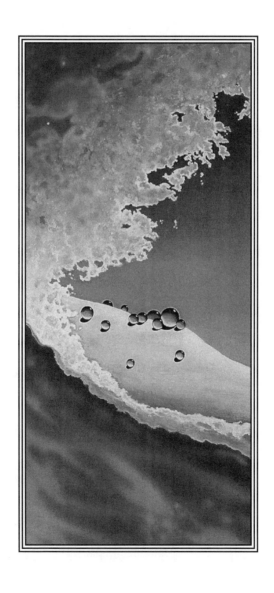

THE ART
OF LETTING GO

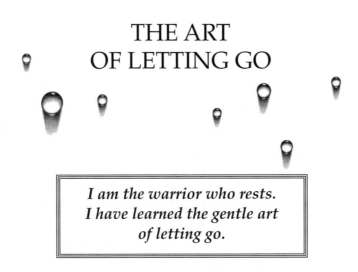

> *I am the warrior who rests.*
> *I have learned the gentle art*
> *of letting go.*

RELEASING THE INVENTORY

The Eagle commands that all human beings take an inventory of the everyday world that they have created for themselves. That inventory is the mechanism of the human mind, the way the first attention watches itself and talks to itself in order to sustain the fixation of the assemblage point in its habitual position. From an energetic viewpoint, the inventory is simply the way the Eagle's emanations focus in on themselves within the structure of our luminous bodies.

In and of itself, the inventory is pure magic. It is a miracle of awareness that helps each of us create a sense of order out of the chaos that surrounds us. In fact, the inventory does its job so well that it eventually tyrannizes us with its effectiveness.

Don Juan tells us that the skimmings of our first attention perceptions are so real and palatable that we are inclined to give them a free hand. This is a terrible error in judgment because when we allow those skimmings to rule us, we lose sight of the fact that these perceptions appear to be real only because it is our own command to perceive them as such.

Warriors *see* that it is the inventory that makes mankind invulnerable, because that is why this self-reflective aspect of awareness came into existence in the first place. In order to establish a corporal awareness, we must maintain a mechanism that effectively separates us from anything beyond the solidity of the world of the tonal.

The Toltecs have shown us that our sense of separateness and invulnerability is nothing more than just plain ignorance and stupidity. Unfortunately, the prevailing social order reinforces this stupidity, because as an organizational construct, it is predicated on the need for the first attention to remain completely separated from the abstract.

In reality, the inventory denies the existence of the unknown so fiercely that for all practical purposes, the nagual simply does not exist as far as it is concerned. This idiosyncrasy of the inventory certainly acts to stabilize our first attention perceptions, but as a consequence it also imprisons us in a world without mystery where we are separated from the magic of *power's promise.*

It is bizarre to realize that this "denial of awareness" lies at the heart of our struggle for empowerment. As human beings, we are conditioned to believe that survival depends on our ability to hold fast to the inventory. After all, it is the inventory that contains all the familiar reference points from which we draw our sense of comfort and security. The inventory is the seat of our self-reflection and the basis for our "sanity" as the social order defines it.

As human beings, we have no choice but to take our inventories, for that is the Eagle's command. And yet as warriors we know that if we worship those inventories, we lose all hope of realizing *power's promise.*

The inventory is an unavoidable fact of life for all human beings, but warriors know that what we do with the inventory once it is taken is entirely up to us. This simple distinction regarding the disposition of the inventory represents the power and the possibility of the warriors who *rest*.

In the final analysis, each of us has the choice to either worship our first attention inventory or discard it. To cling to that inventory and its despotic self-reflection is to choose a comfortable prison of awareness from which there is little chance that we will ever emerge. To release the inventory on the other hand, represents a magical and nurturing act of empowerment. As warriors, we take the most accurate of inventories and then rejoice as we let them go, for that is the way of the *impeccable* action.

DROPPING THINGS FROM OUR LIVES

In order to become empowered as warriors, we learn the gentle art of letting go. Once we release our first attention agendas and the desire to cling to our conditional inventory, we can then can act for the spirit alone. This new and empowered perspective enables us to realize that at any given moment we can drop things from our lives as our *impeccability* dictates.

Convincing ourselves that we have the capacity to release our senseless burdens is a very powerful insight. Those of us who command this viewpoint can gently step away from the things that only separate us from the beacon of *power's promise*.

Don Juan tells us that we each have energetic liens and mortgages that weigh heavily upon us and drain our power. These drains on our energy are the outgrowths of our inventory, the despotic forces of morbidity, obsession and self-importance. It is these terrible liabilities that keep us pinned to the narrow spot of self-reflection and impede our progress on the Toltec path of knowledge.

Most human beings remain immobilized by these familiar burdens, but not so the warriors who *rest*. We free ourselves from their debilitating effects by simply refusing to cling to them. In this way we drop our terrible loads and leave them by the side of the road where they belong.

But as we drop things from our lives, we also recognize the act of release as a strangely double-edged sword, representing both an act of empowerment and a potential threat to the authority of the first attention. The resolution of this contradiction presents a formidable challenge for those on the path of knowledge.

On one hand, we know we must let go of our energetic liabilities if we are to progress towards *power's promise*. One the other hand, we also know that to unburden ourselves in an indiscriminate way can threaten our very existence as human beings. And so as warriors, we are compelled to learn the gentle art of letting go, a strategy of release that reflects both decisiveness and finesse.

THE WARRIORS' FINESSE

Dropping things from our lives is not something that we do arbitrarily or from a perspective of self-importance. Warriors do not drop things as a ploy to avoid responsibility or as a convenient method of stepping out of a difficult situation. When warriors drop things from their lives, they do so because the spirit gives them an indication that it is time for something to be released.

But even when acting under the auspices of the spirit, warriors never drop things with a clatter and a bang. In order to protect the integrity of the tonal, we release things noiselessly so that not even our irascible first attention will become alarmed.

As warriors we define ourselves as individuals committed to an all-out war, but oddly enough our ability to survive the battle depends largely on our capacity for gentleness and finesse. The Toltecs remind us over and over again that warriors who cannot be tender and delicate in the execution of their maneuvers are likely to end up dead.

Don Juan tells us that the warriors' reasons are simple but that their finesse is extreme. In order to accomplish the nearly-impossible tasks of warriorship, we must exercise a gentle artfulness and an exquisite sense of balance that are impossible to describe.

Extreme and excessive behavior tends to either force the tonal into a suicidal plunge or lead to a fatal misstep in the unforgiving world of power. *Impeccable* warriors know the path of knowledge has many pitfalls and that a very special sensitivity is necessary to avoid them.

In many ways this critical finesse can be understood as a function of the warriors' inaccessibility. Power requires that we handle everything in the world lightly, including ourselves. We tap things gently and move away swiftly, leaving hardly a trace of our presence when we are gone.

The capacity for delicacy, gentleness, patience, and forgiveness is the hallmark of *impeccable* warriors, and it is the actualization these qualities that differentiates us from the "telecote." The gentle warriors are the warriors who *rest*, the warriors who succeed in changing everything with a delicate touch that is almost imperceptible.

Gentle warriors are joyful warriors who have no need for harshness in their lives. Gentle warriors are balanced warriors, warriors who find harmony and beauty in the contradictions of awareness. Gentle warriors are fluid warriors, warriors released to the magic of their own finesse.

THE IMMUTABILITY
OF POWER

> *I am the warrior who rests.*
> *I have learned there is*
> *no substitute for resting.*

POWER IS AND POWER MOVES

P ower is and power moves; these are the only things that warriors know for sure. Power is an absolute that exists beyond thoughts or words or deeds. As warriors, we know we can never understand power, we simply become familiar with it through experience. And even after a lifetime of practice, we cannot say that we know what power is.

Don Juan tells us that power is simply something that warriors deal with, an incredible far-fetched affair that is beyond reason and rational comprehension. When we begin our journey of return, we may not have power or even realize that it exists, yet we intuit the presence of something that was not apparent to us before.

As we walk the path to knowledge, power begins to manifest itself as something uncontrollable that comes to us. The forces we are tapping are awesome and overwhelming, and even though we cannot quantify their presence, we experience firsthand the marvelous effects that power places before us.

As warriors, we cannot say how power finds its way to us. All we *see* is that power expresses itself in the world of the tonal as an endless contradiction. Having waited patiently, we wake one day to find that somehow power has been enticed to meet us on the path of knowledge. Suddenly, and without warning, we realize power as something incomprehensible inside us, something that controls our acts and at the same time obeys our commands.

This contradiction of intent is the essence of sorcery, an inexplicable absolute with which warriors learn to flow. From a reasonable standpoint, the whole concept of power and its contradictions is preposterous and impossible. Power is immutable in its conditional inconsistencies, and we will never conform them to our reason. These contradictions are inexplicable by nature and all that we can do is release ourselves to the wonder of their mystery. Power is and power moves; these are the only things that warriors know for sure.

THE CLASH OF THE CONDITIONAL AND THE UNCONDITIONAL

Warriors who *see* clearly, realize that the contradictions of power are not contradictions at all. They are merely the apparent inconsistencies that result when man's first-attention perspective collides head-on with the unalterable nature of power itself.

This mighty clash of conflicting realities throws anyone who encounters it into a dizzying tail-spin. As warriors, the only way to stabilize this all-too-human reaction, is transform our emphasis and relate to the world of power from an ever more *creative* perspective.

The Toltecs have shown us that power can never be coaxed into meeting us on the playing field of reason. Power is unalterable in its incomprehensibility, and when the gap between the conditional and the unconditional is reconciled, it is warriors who build a span to the impossible.

The warriors' *love,* the warriors' *joy,* and warriors' *equilibrium* all contain the essence of a blueprint for such a bridge, but there is no way to access any of these magical plans with the facilities of the mind alone. When a bridge such as this is constructed, it emerges inexplicably from the realm of the nagual.

As warriors who struggle to come to power, we realize that we are wrestling with a mysterious force that can never be rationalized or contained. The only way to sustain the course of our journey of return is to release ourselves to the power of what we cannot know, and seek our *victory* in the contradictory interface of power's most incomprehensible forces.

THE IRREPLACEABILITY OF REST

The Toltecs have shown us that there is only one thing necessary to proceed on the path of knowledge; we must have personal power! The way of the *impeccable* action is paramount for warriors, because it provides us with a strategy for gathering those energetic resources for ourselves. Our battle plan of personal empowerment is simple and straightforward, we make it our unbending intent to *rest.*

Resting is the key to *creative victory,* and the mightiest of the weapons in our warriors' arsenal. It is a magnificent sword, sharp enough to cut down the thousands headed monster of self-importance. It is a powerful steed, ready to carry us over the confining battlements of our stifling conditional inventory. It is a resilient and soothing armor that shields us from the first attention despots that would entice us to open our veins and bleed until we're dry.

Warriors know that there is no substitute for *resting,* because there is no substitute for personal power on the path of knowledge. There is no alternate route to *power's promise,* and without the necessary energy, the journey of return cannot begin.

Resting is the key to an infinite number of avenues to power. It is part of an intensely personal process that leads to the magical threshold of our complete potential. But as we learn to *rest,* we *see* that there is no detailed road map for the mysterious road ahead; each of us must assume responsibility for the individuality of our path by struggling with the intricacies of our own individual fate.

No teacher can lay out our course for us, or show us exactly where to step. Each of us must develop our own intuitive sensibilities and use them to find our way. For as don Juan tells us, as *impeccable* warriors, we already have everything we need to proceed with the most important work of our lives.

In the final analysis, the Toltec path of knowledge leaves us with nothing but our own resources on which to rely, and as warriors, we must be determined to show our mettle in the face of the unknown. We have glimpsed the promise of the indescribable and will not be prevented from our ultimate *creative victory. Freedom* calls and we struggle to respond with a life of *impeccable* action, because in the awesome world of power there simply is no substitute for an empowering life of *rest.*

ALTERNATIVES, POSSIBILITIES AND POTENTIAL

> *I am the warrior who rests.*
> *I have learned that resting is the key*
> *to my unlimited potential.*

THE ONLY DOOR

As warriors we pursue *freedom* by saving our energy and empowering the movement of the assemblage point beyond its habitual location. Don Juan tells us that when this progressive movement extends beyond a certain limit, the result is the assembly of other total worlds. The threshold of this critical movement is called the only door there is.

The only door there is stands between the conditional confinement of the known and the unconditional expanse of the unknown and the unknowable. It is a threshold that opens first to the place of no pity and then beyond to an infinite number of unimaginable new realities.

The movement of the assemblage point away from its habitual position is the essence of the warrior's journey of return, and the Toltecs tell us that this critical movement hinges on the level of our personal power. No man or woman on the path of knowledge can reach their goal without sufficient energy, and therefore, if we cannot implement a comprehensive strategy for the conservation of our energetic resources, then the personal power necessary for the warriors' abstract flight never becomes available to us.

As warriors, we endeavor to live our lives in terms of such a strategy, by battling to break the ties of the black magicians and learning to *rest*. It is our quest for *impeccability* that empowers us and sets us on the road to *freedom*.

And as we travel our path with heart, we become the warriors nurtured and protected and returned to *love*. We conserve, connect and direct ourselves and release our lives to that which cannot be described. And after years of struggle we awake one day to realize that power has lead us to the threshold of the only door there is.

THE PROBABLE, THE POSSIBLE,
AND THE IMPOSSIBLE

As warriors we spend a lifetime empowering ourselves with a clear view of the triumvirate of attention, the *probable*, the *possible* and the *impossible*. In the language of the Toltecs this threesome has many names. They are the known, the unknown, and the unknowable; the first, the second, and the third attentions; the alternatives, the possibilities, and the potential of the human race. Warriors are not satisfied to experience just one or two of these aspects of awareness. Our goal is the total *freedom* that accompanies an awareness of all three.

We all begin life with an ever-solidifying attention of the probable, an awareness of the conditions and expectations of the first attention. As we grow, we come to base our lives on these mechanical *probabilities*, without ever considering the magical *possibilities* that are also open to us.

The first attention dulls us into believing we can assume and expect what the world of solid objects holds for us. Unfortunately, as a result of this misinformed attitude, we close ourselves off to the *possibilities* of anything beyond those boring expectations.

The world of *probabilities* gives us the illusion of living in a comfortable and predictable universe where conditional control and reactions keep us safe. But in reality it is only a world of our own creation, a comfortable and familiar prison filled with victims of self-importance.

The residents of this sterile and familiar universe are resigned to bleed together, and they debilitate themselves in acts of needless self-destruction. But the Toltecs have *seen* that when we bleed, all we ever do is bleed alone, wasting the precious energy that could carry us to new levels of attention.

As warriors, we have glimpsed the promise that waits for us and we will not be contained. We choose to build our lives, not around the reasonable *probabilities* that direct the course of most lives, but around the *possibilities* and *impossibilities* that wait for us beyond the limits of the known.

Warriorship empowers us and makes possible the emergence of a new *creative attention.* As this remarkable awareness solidifies, the *probable* no longer confines us. We have contacted the hidden power beyond our superficial alternatives, and are now focused on all that is *possible* in our lives. Warriors realize that all things are within the reach of the luminous beings, including that which is not *probable* at all.

Possibilities and *impossibilities* now form the core of a brave new continuity that has been verified by our own sorcery experience. The Toltec path of knowledge enables us to transcend many aspects of our everyday lives, including the boring sterility of our own first attention *probabilities* and expectations.

IMPECCABILITY AND
THE WARRIORS' POTENTIAL

I t is the promise of the warriors' potential that beckons us to merge with the abstract in a state of total awareness. The Toltecs tell us that *impeccability* is the key to this potential; that by actualizing the way of the *impeccable* action, we can push past the limits of the *probable* into the realm of what is *possible* and even *impossible* for the average individual.

The further we push into this uncharted territory, the closer we come to the realization of *power's promise*. In Toltec terms, this incomprehensibility is called the unknowable or the third attention. It is an immeasurable consciousness beyond the first and second rings of power, a consciousness that engages incomprehensible aspects of awareness.

Don Juan defines the third attention as total awareness, the totality of the self, or total *freedom*. The attainment of this awareness is a somersault of thought into the inconceivable, the realization of *power's promise*, and the fulfillment of the warriors' *impeccable* bid for power.

One thing and one thing only will carry us to that *impossible* destination, beyond the *probabilities* and *possibilities* on the path of knowledge. One thing and one thing only will enable us to maintain our *equilibrium* and overcome the pitfalls that wait along the avenue of power. One thing and one thing only will help us harmonize the forces of warriorship and sorcery as we face the inorganics in their realm. One thing and one thing only will sustain us on our lifelong journey of return, until the triumphant moment when we burn with the luminous fire from within.

This one empowering tool is our *impeccability,* our irreplaceable ability to establish and maintain a critical level of personal power. It is *resting* alone that poises us on the Toltec path of knowledge and eventually sustains the realization of our most *impossible* potential.

Part Ten
The Promise Always Kept

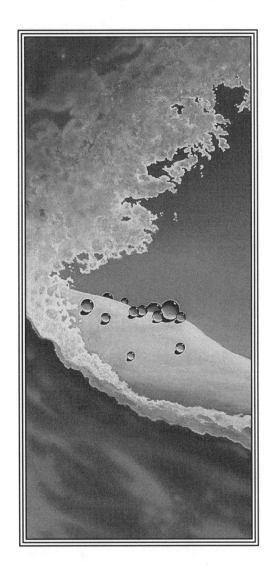

THE DESIGNS
OF POWER

> *All things come
> to the warrior who rests.*

POWER REINFORCES ITSELF

Power is and power moves. These are the only things that warriors know for sure. Power flows of its own accord and we can never hope to understand its workings. Even when power finally comes to us, we cannot say how or why it has arrived. The flow of power is an enigma of impossible proportions, it washes over us like a wave and leaves us breathless.

Power is an absolute that cannot be contained or described in words. We understand that power is beyond us and that the most we can do is become familiar with it through firsthand experience.

The warrior-sorcerers' contact with the spirit leads to the silent knowledge that power always acts to reinforce itself. Even if its designs seem contradictory on a first attention level, we *see* that power is completely consistent with regard to itself.

Even warriors cannot predict how this magical reinforcement will occur. We cannot understand how power manifests itself, nor can we say that it would have flowed to us more easily if the conditions of our lives had been different. The ephemeral designs of power are incomprehensible in every respect, including the way they act to reinforce themselves.

THE FLOW OF POWER

T he flow of power is a clear reflection of an absolute that exists far beyond all limits and confines of human comprehension. The way the spirit moves is the expression of an unalterable truth, and it is our relationship to that flow that determines either our empowerment or debilitation.

The Toltecs have shown us that the process of nurturing ourselves is simply a matter of flowing with power in the best of all possible fashions. Power is limitless and enigmatic, and in order to tap its awesome potential, we must learn to open ourselves to the unfathomable agenda of its often contradictory designs.

To ignore or resist this unalterable reality is nothing short of sheer idiocy, since remaining disconnected from the flow of power only acts to separate us from our own unlimited potential. The spirit prompts us daily with indications designed to put us in sync with its movements, because power always acts to reinforce itself. Warriors understand that in its own incomprehensible way, power is constantly steering every human being back toward the abstract source to which we are all so intimately connected.

It is the first attention that conditions us to often act in opposition to the flow of power. The disconnected perspective of the individual self refuses to allow for an awareness of anything beyond itself, and this is its fatal flaw. Don Juan tells us that the only advantage we have is the scope of our own awareness, and it is up to us to expand our perception beyond its familiar limits.

The warriors' trick is to escape the tyranny of the attention of the tonal and simply flow with power. We open ourselves to an awareness of intent and release ourselves willingly to it, trusting in it above all other things. The despots of the first attention are then no longer capable of leading us upstream in opposition to power's natural movements. As warriors, we are fluid and free, directing ourselves with the natural indications of the spirit, and our inborn intuition and intent.

Once we release ourselves to the beacon of the nagual, living with the rhythm of power becomes a natural way of being. In Toltec terms this lifestyle is called the way of the *impeccable* action. *Resting* enables us to stop the madness of the way we were before. Instead of bleeding ourselves dry with senseless acts of cynical self-destruction, we choose proactivity and the empowering path to *freedom*. Instead of living within the confines of our own self-obsessed expectations, we flow with power and navigate our way to an emerging *creative victory*.

THE CONFRONTATION
WITH POWER

The warriors who *rest* are the warriors who flow with power and accept the incomprehensibility of its designs. We are the warriors transformed, the warriors who allow power to act as our navigational guide. We are the warriors who *see* clearly, the warriors in tune with the edifice of intent.

But ironically, the more we confront the reality of power, the more vulnerable we become to its sheer intensity. Suddenly, that which we have fought so hard to open ourselves to, emerges as our most formidable enemy. As warriors, we know we have no choice but to confront this awesome adversary in order to prevent it from vanquishing us.

The Toltecs tell us that we must face a series of four natural enemies on the path of knowledge. The first is fear, the second is clarity, and the third is power, itself. As the warriors who *rest*, we overcome our first two enemies with sheer guts and intuition. But the third enemy of the warrior is a much more insidious foe, it doesn't even appear to be an adversary!

Warriors reach a point where power has come to us and we can do with it whatever we please. We have learned to *see* and it is possible for us to command the power of our will. We seem to have become invulnerable, because our wish is now the rule. But in reality all we have done is confront ourselves with our greatest challenge.

Don Juan tells us that power is the most overwhelming of all our enemies because the easiest thing to do is to give in to it. Power makes us feel truly invincible, and if we aren't totally alert, we will awake one day to find that we have suddenly lost the game.

Those who lose the battle with power are no longer warriors at all. They have abandoned the quest for *freedom* and resigned themselves to become cruel and capricious human beings.

Warriors defeated by power cannot continue on their path to *victory*, and die not knowing how to handle that which has found its way to them. The Toltecs tell us that power can only be a burden for those incapable of maintaining an appropriate level of command over themselves. Unless we empty ourselves sufficiently, the acquisition of all things becomes nothing more than a morbid obsession. There is no *victory* in such a life, only the poignancy of a magical promise now flown by.

THE WARRIORS
WHO WAIT

> *And all things become nothing*
> *for the warrior who waits.*

WAITING FOR
THE BLUEPRINT OF POWER

As warriors on the road to power, we understand that we must someday build an unimaginable bridge, a bridge that will connect the first and second rings of power and return us to the limitlessness of the abstract.

The blueprint for this magical bridge is elusive and invisible. As warriors we cannot read or study it with the resources of our minds. Instead we must trust that we will access it directly through a process beyond our conscious control. For the warrior's blueprint of power lies hidden in the immensity of the abstract, far beyond the conditional capacities of reason, language and deliberate action.

Yet in spite of its incomprehensible qualities, we wait for the minimal chance that this magical blueprint may materialize for us within our lifetimes. And while we wait, we practice the art of *resting*. Our *impeccable* demeanor empowers and nurtures us. Our cleansing breaths clear our vision and enable us to choose well. The conservation of our precious energy empowers us to direct our lives with our intuition and our intent. Our warriors' facade is rearranged as we reshape ourselves and shatter the mirror of our own self-reflection.

And as we *rest*, our incomprehensible transformation begins. We reorder ourselves and find peace in a *creative victory* without reward. We free ourselves by abandoning the agendas of the first attention for the unfathomable agenda of power. As the warriors transformed we joyfully walk our personal path with heart, and as we travel, the petty things we once clung to are now released in an *impeccable* act of letting go.

Our magical alteration changes us from reactive objects in a world of circumstance to proactive beings in a world of power. Instead of being drained by the demands of the first attention, we empower ourselves through an ever-strengthening link with intent. Instead of remaining victims, we reconnect with our own strength and hidden resources. Instead of being pinned down within the boundaries of the tonal, we dare to break the very barrier of our own perception.

And if one day we wake to find that the magical blueprint of power has found its way to us, then we will become the warrior architects, poised to complete an impossible bridge across forever. The bridge we build with the power at our service will vault our attention beyond its limits to the seat of an unalterable reality where all contradictions are reconciled, a position of the assemblage point where the tonal and the nagual coexist in the same instant. All things will now have come to us, but in our humility and our detachment, they will seem as nothing.

COMMANDING THE WILL

As warriors for total *freedom*, we know that we are waiting and we know what we are waiting for.

Those of us on the path of knowledge wait patiently for our will.

We know that will does not become available to us until we have accumulated a great surplus of energy, so while we gather our personal power, warriors learn to patiently wait. And if one day our *impeccability* entices our will to finally emerge, then we will find ourselves in command of all things possible.

Will is a center of assemblage through which it is possible to access and use the extraordinary effects of the nagual. Will is a power that has to be controlled and tuned, it is the mysterious force that assembles the warrior. Will is a level of proficiency, a state of being that comes abruptly to warriors according to the incomprehensible designs of power.

When warriors acquire will, it can be said that they have acquired everything, even though the acquisition of will goes superficially unnoticed. Will is quiet and unobtrusive, yet it is staggering in its capacity to channel the energy of the warrior's total being to produce anything within the boundaries of possibility.

Will is a power within us, it is not an object or a thought or a wish. It is the power that makes warriors invulnerable, the force that allows us to succeed when our thoughts tell us we are defeated. Will is what carries warriors over the conditional walls of the first attention, walls that confine the average individual for an entire lifetime.

Will is what sends warriors literally through a wooden door or to the surface of the moon, it is the power of the second attention to focus on anything we want. But by the time we have acquired will, we have also lost the need to use it in equal measure. As truly *impeccable* individuals, we are like intent itself, we have no conditional needs or desires.

We are the warriors who *rest,* the selfless *creative victors* who have released ourselves to power in order to become airborne, fluid, and free. Now we employ our power, but only as power itself directs. For commanding the will is not something we accomplish from a self-involved perspective. In the lives of *impeccable* warriors, power only acts to reinforce itself.

EVERYTHING AND NOTHING

A s warriors we are content to relinquish our conditional agendas because we have *seen* that all things are equal and unimportant. For us, everything is filled to the brim because our *creative attention* infuses the items of our world with the power of the impossible.

Our strength and *impeccability* support a life that is filled with unconditional *love, joy,* and *equilibrium.* We live the contradiction between everything and nothing, we connect ourselves to everything important by emptying ourselves to nothing.

The everything that warriors attain has nothing to do with the acquisition of things or the selfish control of others. In the world of power, there is no conditional victory or defeat, there is no ego or sense of superiority. For warriors there is only a sense that life is bursting with possibilities and that our *impeccable* struggle is surely worth our while.

The warriors who wait have gained everything by losing everything. Our battle with the personal self has empowered us and led us to the acquisition of all things. In turn our death has advised us that we have already lost everything and therefore we have nothing to fear.

As waiting warriors we have experienced the true meaning of everything and nothing. Our ability to *see* has shown us that nothing really matters because the same unalterable truth is equally reflected in everything around us. The quest for *power's promise* has led us to the understanding that our only real task is to prepare ourselves to be aware.

By emptying ourselves and becoming nothing we accomplish the incomprehensible *not-doing* of our impossible objective. For only when we become nothing can we possibly hope to become everything.

THE WARRIORS'
DESTINY

> ### The promise of power
> ### is the promise always kept.

THE PROMISE ALWAYS MADE

The *promise of power* is the promise always made, a universal promise that is infinite and unalterable. It is tragic to realize that for most men and women this magical covenant is a promise totally ignored.

Don Juan tells us that the great fallacy of human kind is to completely disregard its connection with intent. Average individuals become so involved and so absorbed in the self-possessed *doings* of the first attention that they never deal with themselves as beings made of energy.

Most people refuse to consider the energetic consequences of their actions and their attitudes. They never realize how they keep themselves pinned down with the consistent and senseless waste of their personal power. Average people trap themselves in a world of reactive victims because they refuse to see beyond the comfortable and familiar confines of the world they have created.

When it comes to *power's promise*, most men and women are just plain unaware. In fact, don Juan tells us that our plight as human beings is the counterpoint between our ignorance and our stupidity. This powerful combination of factors produces a tremendously debilitating state of mind that prevents us from recognizing the glimmers of our unlimited potential.

It is stupidity which forces us to disregard anything that does not conform to our self-reflective expectations. From the Toltec perspective, this means that our power of our stupidity is directly proportional to the degree to which we allow the first attention self to "tunnel us in" on the description of the world.

As warriors, we insist on demeaning our stupidity by coming to understand it. We refuse to allow the well-intentioned programming of the first attention to rule our awareness, so we confront it and assume responsibility for the rearrangement of its emphasis.

It is the way of the *impeccable* action that gives us the courage and energetic resources to shatter our self-reflective mirror. The Toltecs have shown us how a life of *rest* empowers us to establish a new perspective where stupidity cannot prevail. This *process of power* is the warriors' salvation, a way of transcending our abysmal ignorance in favor of the promise always made.

THE PROMISE ALWAYS KEPT

W arriors *see* that the promise always made is also the promise always kept. This unalterable fact is difficult for most people to accept because in the world of the first attention there are so many superficial differences between individuals and their fates.

But as warriors we know there is no destiny, there is only power's universal promise. No matter what the individual conditions of our lives may seem to be, the spirit maintains its unconditional covenant with each and every one of us as luminous beings.

Power is an impossible contradiction, an unalterable affair whose movements cannot be understood by anyone. Despite the apparent variations between the people who share our lives, the only real difference between any of us is that some of us are more aware than others. There is no right or wrong, or good or bad, at the heart of this distinction, there is only an incomprehensible promise made and an incomprehensible promise kept.

From the Toltec perspective, it is pointless to consume our energy contemplating our circumstantial fate as warrior-sorcerers. Whatever happens regarding our *impeccable* bid for power, we understand that we will not fulfill our conditional destiny because there is no conditional destiny to fulfill. All we can do is release ourselves to the unconditional mystery of the universe, and prepare ourselves for the day when power will engulf us in the miraculous realization of the promise always kept.

THE REALIZATION OF THE PROMISE

One pragmatic message of the Toltec warriors' dialogue is that the human race is capable of evolving if we succeed in changing the social base of our perception. In other words, if we learn to shift our emphasis away from an obsession with the self-centered *probabilities* of the first attention, then we can open ourselves to the limitless *possibilities* and *impossibilities* of the second and third attentions.

In order to do this, we must be exposed to ideas that will pull us away from the outer world and reconnect us with the inner world of the abstract. Once given the minimal chance to realize the mysteries that seers have uncovered, it is then possible for each of us to abstract ourselves through a life of practicing warriorship and sorcery.

The inspirational message of nagualism is the simple articulation of *power's promise* and the empirical assurance that this promise is always made and always kept. The Toltecs have inspired us by reminding us of what we already know in the recesses of our being. But these warrior-sorcerers do more than just talk a good line. They have exceeded the limits of their own inspiration by actually demonstrating that merging with the unalterable in a state of total awareness is an attainable goal.

Mankind is capable of evolving, and power always acts to reinforce itself! Once we free our consciousness from the bindings of the social order, it is intent, itself, that will redirect our awareness onto a new and *impossible* path! The new seers of don Juan's Toltec lineage are living proof that this miraculous evolution of awareness can be accomplished.

DENOUEMENT

THE LIMITS OF INSPIRATION

The Toltec experience serves as a beacon of spiritual inspiration for many complex reasons. The written record of nagualism illuminates an indescribable aspect of our being and touches us in ways that are not comprehensible to our minds. The warriors' dialogue entices us with inklings of an elusive and invisible presence, an intangible reality which despite its ephemeral nature, cannot be completely denied by the unwitting tyranny of the first attention.

For anyone open to the manifestations of the spirit, the beacon of nagualism reminds us of what we already silently know. It beckons us to remember ourselves in spite of our own stupidity, and challenges us to complete a journey of return through the realization of our long-secreted potential.

But the dialogue of the Toltec warriors inspires us for the simplest and most profound of reasons. The record of their successful bid for power engages our innermost attention because on some subliminal level, each of us knows that the unfathomable path to *freedom* is as real as real can be.

It is nearly incomprehensible to realize what the new seers have accomplished. These *impeccable* warrior-sorcerers have outlined the essence of a path to the threshold of power itself! They have carried the realization of *power's promise* beyond the flaw with words, and actualized it as an empirical aspect of the human experience!

These soldiers of the third attention have accomplished a miraculous journey that every human being longs to make. They have returned to the abstract in a state of total awareness. They have burned with the fire from within and flown into eternity on the incomprehensible wings of intent.

And yet despite the scope of their attainment, these *impeccable* warriors cannot lead us bodily to *freedom*. The Toltecs can inspire us by redefining what is possible for the human race, but beyond that they hold no salvation for us as individuals. In order to come to knowledge, power demands that each of us struggle by ourselves on a very personal and private battlefield.

As warriors we must revive our spirit and tackle everything for ourselves. The Toltecs' example serves as an informational and intuitive template for the road that we must travel, but that is all it can ever do. The ultimate *creative victory* of the new seers can serve as our spiritual inspiration, but it can never stand as a substitute for the power of our own experience!

In order to accept the Eagle's gift, we must assume responsibility for our own energetic condition and summon the courage to actualize our intent! If nothing else, the Toltecs have shown us that the individual realization of our evolutionary potential is an ultra personal process that has no shortcuts.

True knowledge cannot be handed down without a struggle, it must be claimed by individuals as their own. Whatever the new seers have accomplished, the example of their attainments means nothing unless it is transformed by practicing warrior-sorcerers into a highly personal process of empowerment and transcendence.

Warriors understand that the informational and intuitive glimmer of nagualism belongs to the *preamble of power,* and that *victory* becomes possible only when that theoretical construct is superseded by an empirical *process of power.* For the true power of nagualism lies in the transcendence of its invigorating message, in our own ability to transcend the limits of spiritual inspiration.

HAVING TO BELIEVE

D on Juan tells us that warriors *have* to believe as an expression of their innermost predilection. They do this as a choice, as an *impeccable* response to their intuition and their intent. Warriors are individuals in touch with the spirit, and as such, they *have* to believe without believing.

In the course of my life there have been many things in which I have *had* to believe. Not the least of these is that there is some reason why a written record of nagualism has come to the fore, despite the selfless indifference of the warriors who *rest.* Power's agenda with regard to the collected work of Carlos Castaneda will never be clear to anyone, and yet I *have* to believe that the availability of this material plays some part in power's own design.

On a much more personal note, I also *have* to believe that there is some reason why the sentences of this and several other books have arranged themselves under my hand and found their way into print. The momentum which has overtaken me is beyond my comprehension, and on some level I continue to resist it based on what I "think" I know about the Toltec path of knowledge.

Not only have I resisted the assembly of these commentaries, for a time I flatly refused to participate in their development. Eventually, however, *impeccability* forced me to override the foolishness of my arbitrary stance, and release myself to the incomprehensible momentum of these projects in the most graceful way I could.

These are the contradictions of my own experience, incongruities that I wrestle with to this very day. I cannot comment other than to say that I have *seen* that I am destined to remain a fool until the moment that I draw my last breath.

A teacher of mine once told me: "Power is and power moves; these are the only things that warriors know for sure." Speaking from personal experience, I can truthfully say that it is impossible to predict what the spirit has in store for any of us. My life has taken many strange and contradictory turns over the years, and to this day I still struggle to release my assumptions and expectations while remaining humble in the face of power.

When all is said and done, I suppose this is the only way that life can ever be. All any of us can ever do is release ourselves to magic and trust in what we *have* to believe. I have *seen* that reason and analysis cannot guide us where we need to go. It is intuition and *impeccability* that will always dictate the road that we are meant to follow.

We must summon the courage to set our foolish agendas aside and release ourselves to power, no matter how its inexplicable designs compare to what we think is called for in any given situation. And so regardless of what we assume and what we expect, each of us *has* to believe that all things in the world around us exist as power itself intends.

A FOOL REMAINS A FOOL

For reasons I cannot begin to grasp, I currently find myself facilitating a group of books that passionately advocate the fundamental message of the Toltec warriors' dialogue. The reader might assume that this turn of events would be a pleasant and natural outgrowth of my involvement with nagualism, but in reality, this could not be further from the truth.

In 1989 I began a period in my life that resulted in the eventual publishing of a concordance to the Toltec warriors' dialogue. The unlikely events surrounding the emergence of that book (and the works that have followed since) have rocked me to my foundations and forced me to re-examine everything I thought I had begun to internalize about warriorship and the way of the *impeccable* action.

There was a time just a few short years ago when I thought I had a firm grasp on what it meant to be a warrior. This perspective encompassed my opinions on many things, including my intensely personal feelings regarding the "Catalog of One Thousand Secrets" that I had so faithfully prepared over a period of more than fifteen years.

Needless to say, power proved me wrong about everything that I thought I knew regarding these things. Before my eyes (and at times literally against my will), my personal concordance to the warriors' dialogue transformed itself into several drafts of a manuscript that was eventually titled *The Promise of Power*. In addition (and without any conscious intervention on my part), an entire group of talented professionals found their way to the project as it evolved, and choose to tirelessly dedicate themselves to the imposing task of bringing this complex reference guide to print.

I completed my direct involvement with *The Promise of Power* in 1993, and it wasn't until years later that the book was finally published. During that interim, a whole new series of inexplicable events overtook my life and led me to facilitate this and several other manuscripts on the Toltec perspective.

The reader must understand that all these things remain incredulous to me. I never intended to become a commentator on the warriors' dialogue, nor do I think that nagualism requires any work like this to represent its viewpoint.

And yet here I sit with my friends the trees who joke with me about how power has moved in spite of my preconceptions and my intellectual resistance. In the face of such events, there is nothing more for an *impeccable* warrior to say than, "So be it!"

I have learned the hard way that no matter what clarity I think I gain, nothing will ever equip me to unravel the designs of the spirit. As long as I walk this living planet, I am destined to remain a fool.

THE BALANCE OF POWER

It is essential for those of us on the path of knowledge to focus on two critical aspects of the Toltec *process of power*. One is the incremental development process through which we become practicing warriors and sorcerers, and the other is our emerging ability to balance the conflicting forces inherent to those divergent disciplines.

In some respects, the latter becomes our most essential skill, for as don Juan reminds us, warriors must learn to balance themselves and the forces around them in order to meet the fundamental challenges of the journey of return. The harmony of the warrior-sorcerer reflects the harmony of the warriors' way, first the balance between actions and decisions, and then the balance between the tonal and the nagual.

It is odd to realize that to some minimal extent, we have all been exercising this marvelous sense of balance since the day that we were born. It is only as we actualize the principles of warriorship and sorcery to ever-greater degrees that the art of balancing becomes increasingly critical to the attainment of our *freedom*.

The *process of power* is a process that reinforces itself, and so does the *art of balancing*. The Toltecs have shown us it is not sufficient to simply trade the realm of the warrior for the realm of the sorcerer. In order to find *freedom* we must create a personal counterpoint between the contradictions of warriorship and sorcery. We must harmonize the dynamic tension between these incongruous forces and use the resulting *equilibrium* as a bridge to our ultimate *creative victory!*

THE WARRIOR-SORCERERS' CREATIVE VICTORY

This book addresses the way that, with only our personal resources in hand, we set out to transform the *preamble of power* into a life of practicing warriorship and sorcery. From any rational perspective, this is a ludicrous task that no one in their right mind would dare to undertake.

That is why the Toltecs have shown us that we can only come to the path of knowledge through the subterfuge and trickery of the spirit. The warriors of the third attention are never volunteers, they are recruited through the incomprehensible auspices of the spirit itself.

But even those of us who find our way to the avenue of power still face a monumental problem. We are human beings, and, as such, we are dependent, craving someone else to guide us along our way. We cling to the intellectual *preamble of power* and what it is we think we know.

How sad that we refuse to believe in our tremendous hidden power. How tragic that most of us remain unwilling to accept that we need so little to get on with the most essential work of our lives.

But get on with it we must, because otherwise nothing in our self-reflective world will ever change. Once touched by *power's preamble* we must use those principles as a template for a life of *impeccable* action. We must empower our way beyond thoughts and words to the practicing realm of the *creative victor*.

For this fool, the term *creative victory* beautifully describes the experience of the realized warrior-sorcerer, a miraculous state of being that gradually emerges from between the contradictions of knowledge in order to light the way to power's promise. This empowered *equilibrium* of the Toltecs is a waking reminder of our luminous totality, a triumphant reflection of what we are and what we have always been. And until the moment when we finally find our *freedom*, it is this interim *creative victory* that will sustain us as we practice the arts of warriorship and sorcery and wait for the designs of power to be revealed.

GLOSSARY OF TERMS

Editor's note: The following glossary will provide the reader with a quick overview of the basic terms used throughout Creative Victory. *Although drawn directly from the Toltec warriors' dialogue, the definitions given here are abbreviated at best, and should not be used as anything more than a preliminary starting point for the serious student. Much more extensive descriptions of these and thousands of other cross-referenced terms can be found in the "Catalog of One Thousand Secrets" section of* The Promise of Power *(the author's concordance to the warriors' dialogue), along with innumerable references to specific relevant passages within the Castaneda books themselves.*

ABANDON-[ABANDON]: Warriors know they must live their lives with impeccable abandon; the warriors' ability to create a gesture for the spirit; the warriors' ability to let go of first attention agendas and concerns.

ABANDON-REFUSAL-[THE REFUSAL TO ABANDON ONESELF]: Warriors know they must refuse to give up or abandon themselves to anything but power itself; the warriors' determination to struggle against all odds; a reflection of the warriors' spirit.

ABERRATION-MORBIDITY-[ABERRATION AND MORBIDITY]: Warriors know that aberration and morbidity are the inherent pitfalls of the path of knowledge; the misdirection of knowledge and power resulting from an individual's inability to resolve the issues of self-importance and self-indulgence.

ABSTRACT-THE-[THE ABSTRACT]: Warriors define the abstract as the force which sustains the universe; the spirit; the nagual; intent; the indescribable; the element that propels the warrior.

ABSTRACT-TO-[TO ABSTRACT ONESELF]: Warriors know they must abstract themselves by making themselves accessible to power and by becoming aware of intent; warriors overcome their feelings of self-importance, and as a result, their sense of self becomes abstract and impersonal; warriors must take every available opportunity to abstract themselves; the warriors' journey is a journey of return to the abstract.

ABSTRACT-RETURN-[A RETURN TO THE ABSTRACT]: Warriors know they must strive to return to the abstract; the return to silent knowledge; the return to intent; the warriors' victorious return to the spirit.

ACCOUNT-SPIRIT-MAN-[PAYING BACK TO THE ACCOUNT OF THE SPIRIT OF MANKIND]: SEE: MAN-SPIRIT-ACCOUNT-[PAYING BACK TO THE ACCOUNT OF THE SPIRIT OF MANKIND]

ACQUIESCENCE: SEE: WARRIOR-ACQUIESCENCE-[THE WARRIORS' ACQUIESCENCE]

ACT-LEARNING-[LEARNING TO ACT]: Warriors know they must learn to act for the spirit; the exercise of controlled folly; to act without expecting rewards or anything else in return; to act just for the hell of it.

ACTING-VS-TALKING-[ACTING VS TALKING]: Warriors know that the difference between acting and talking is the difference between the worlds of the tonal and the nagual; in the world of the tonal the warrior talks; in the world of the nagual the warrior acts.

ACTING-VS-THINKING-[ACTING VS THINKING]: Warriors learn to act instead of thinking too much about acting, or thinking about their actions once they have acted; warriors only have problems understanding the spirit when they think about it; when they act, the spirit easily reveals itself to them.

AIRBORNE-[AIRBORNE]: SEE: WARRIOR-AIRBORNE-[AIRBORNE WARRIORS]

ALIGNMENT-[ALIGNMENT]: Warriors know that alignment is the phenomenon which allows awareness to be cultivated by living creatures; the force that leads to perception; the unique force that either keeps the assemblage point stationary or helps make it shift.

ARTIFICE-SUBTERFUGE-[ARTIFICE AND SUBTERFUGE]: Warriors know that artifice and subterfuge lie at the core of the teaching method of nagualism; the subterfuge and trickery of the spirit.

ARTS-WARRIOR-[THE WARRIORS' ARTS]: SEE: WARRIOR-ARTS-[THE WARRIORS' ARTS]

ASSEMBLAGE-POINT-[THE ASSEMBLAGE POINT]: Warriors know that the assemblage point is the place where perception is assembled within the structure of mankind's luminous cocoon.

ASSEMBLAGE-POINT-MOVING-[MOVING THE ASSEMBLAGE POINT]: Warriors know that it is possible for the assemblage point to move; the warriors' ability to allow the spirit to move the assemblage point from its usual position on the surface of the luminous cocoon to another position, either on the surface, into the luminous interior, or outside the luminous cocoon.

ASSEMBLAGE-POINT-SECRETS-[THE SECRETS OF THE ASSEMBLAGE-POINT]: Warriors know that now, more than ever, mankind needs to be taught the secrets of the assemblage point.

ASSUMPTIONS: SEE EXPECTATION-[EXPECTATION]

ATTENTION-[ATTENTION]: Warriors know that attention is that with which we hold our images of the world; attention is the harnessing and enhancing of awareness through the process of being alive; attention has three levels of attainment, three independent domains, the first, the second and the third attentions.

ATTENTION-FIRST-[THE FIRST ATTENTION]: Warriors know that the first attention is the utilization of emphasized emanations from the narrow band where mankind's awareness is normally located; the glow of awareness fixed on the surface of mankind's luminous cocoon; the right side; normal awareness; the tonal; this world of solid objects; the known; the attention of the tonal.

ATTENTION-NAGUAL-[THE ATTENTION OF THE NAGUAL]: Warriors know that the attention of the nagual is the second attention; the second ring of power; the warriors' capacity to place awareness on the non-ordinary world; the attention under the table.

ATTENTION-SECOND-[THE SECOND ATTENTION]: Warriors know that the second attention is the utilization of normally unused emanations inside mankind's luminous cocoon; a more specialized state of the glow of awareness resulting from the utilization of unused emanations inside mankind's luminous cocoon; left side awareness; the nagual; the other world; the unknown; the attention of the nagual; the battlefield of the warrior; the training ground for the third attention.

ATTENTION-THIRD-[THE THIRD ATTENTION]: Warriors know that the third attention is the largest portion of attention; an immeasurable consciousness that engages undefinable aspects of awareness.

ATTENTION-TONAL-[THE ATTENTION OF THE TONAL]: Warriors know that the attention of the tonal is the first attention; the first ring of power; the capacity of average people to place their awareness on the ordinary world of common sense and solid objects; the attention over the table.

AWARENESS-[AWARENESS]: Warriors know that awareness is a glow in the cocoon of a living being which is more intense than the rest of its luminous structure.

AWARENESS-NORMAL-[NORMAL AWARENESS]: Warriors know that mankind's normal state of awareness is the world of solid objects; the known; the first attention; the attention of the tonal.

AWARENESS-SUBLIMINAL-[THE SUBLIMINAL AWARENESS OF OUR POSSIBILITIES]: Warriors know that men and women are subliminally aware of their complete potential.

AWARENESS-SURROGATE-[THE WARRIORS' SURROGATE AWARENESS]: Warriors know that they can create a replica of awareness through a perfect recapitulation; the warriors of the new cycle use their surrogate awareness to dart past the Eagle to freedom.

AWARENESS-TOTAL-[TOTAL AWARENESS]: Warriors know that total awareness is the culmination of the warriors' search for total freedom; the ultimate bastion of awareness.

AWARENESS-TRUTHS-[THE TRUTHS ABOUT AWARENESS]: Warriors know that the truths about awareness are certain conclusions reached through *seeing* about the nature of mankind and the world; the explanation of awareness.

AWARENESS-WE-ARE-[WE ARE AN AWARENESS]: Warriors know that they are an awareness, that they are perceivers; warriors know they are boundless and not solid objects.

BALANCE-[BALANCE]: Warriors know that they begin life with their spirits somewhat off balance and that they must spend a lifetime doing their ultimate best to regain that balance; the balance and harmony of the warriors' way.

BEAUTY-[BEAUTY]: Warriors know that they must develop a peculiar appreciation for beauty; they lavish beauty on those around them, retaining for themselves only their longing; this shock of beauty is called stalking; the warriors' sense of beauty is part of their sobriety, it distinguishes warriors from those who have been aberrated by their contact with power.

BELIEVE-HAVING-TO-[HAVING TO BELIEVE]: Warriors know they must evolve a specific perspective on believing; they do this as a choice, as an expression of their innermost predilection; the warriors' secret of believing is that they believe without believing.

BIRD-FREEDOM-[THE BIRD OF FREEDOM]: Warriors speak of the path of knowledge as a magical, mysterious bird which pauses in its flight for a moment in order to give mankind hope and purpose; warriors live under the wing of that bird, which is called the bird of freedom; warriors nourish that bird with their dedication and impeccability; the bird of freedom always flies in a straight line, it can never circle back; the bird of freedom can do only two things, take warriors along or leave them behind.

BLACK-MAGICIANS-[THE BLACK MAGICIANS]: Warriors know that the black magicians are our fellow men and women; those who would keep warriors tied down with their thoughts and first attention agendas.

BLEEDING-TOGETHER-[WE ARE BLEEDING TOGETHER]: SEE: DAGGER-METAPHORICAL-[THE METAPHORICAL DAGGER]

BOREDOM-[BOREDOM]: Warriors know that they must turn their backs on boredom, the boredom of the first attention's limited description of the world.

BOUNDARIES-AFFECTION-[THE BOUNDARIES OF AFFECTION]: Warriors know that their feelings make boundaries around everything; these are the boundaries of affection; the stronger the feeling, the stronger the boundary.

BOUNDARIES-SELF-[THE BOUNDARIES OF THE INDIVIDUAL SELF]: Warriors use the recapitulation to transcend the narrow boundaries of their person; when the recapitulation is complete, warriors no longer abide by the limitations of the personal self.

BREATH-[BREATH]: Warriors know that breath is a magical life-giving function with a cleansing capacity; breath is the key element in the warriors' recapitulation; breathing is a magical life-giving act, a vehicle for the warriors' energy when used in conjunction with the warriors' recapitulation; the exhalation of a breath ejects foreign energy from the body while the inhalation pulls back energy that has been left behind.

BRIDGE-[THE WARRIORS' BRIDGE]: SEE: WARRIOR-BRIDGE-[THE WARRIORS' BRIDGE]

BUSINESS-DOWN-TO-[GETTING DOWN TO BUSINESS]: Warriors know there is only one way to learn, and that is to get down to business; to talk about power is useless, warriors must tackle everything themselves.

CARING-[CARING FOR ANOTHER]: SEE: WARRIOR-CARING-FOR-ANOTHER-[CARING FOR ANOTHER WARRIOR]

CARLOS CASTANEDA-[CARLOS CASTANEDA]: A new-age author who continues to chronicle the Toltec warriors' dialogue through his writings; Carlos is an apprentice to the nagual Juan Matus, and a three-pronged nagual himself; to date he has published nine books on nagualism.

CHANCE-HAVE-[A CHANCE TO HAVE A CHANCE]: Warriors know that the Eagle's gift it is not a bestowal but a chance to have a chance for freedom.

CHANCE-MINIMAL-[THE MINIMAL CHANCE]: SEE: WARRIOR-CHANCE-MINIMAL-[THE WARRIORS' MINIMAL CHANCE]:

CHANGE-[CHANGE]: Warriors know they must struggle to change themselves, to transform the island of the tonal by altering rather than obliterating the use of its assigned elements; warriors change their idea of the world; the contradiction of change is that no matter how warriors struggle to change themselves, they are still no more than luminous beings and there is nothing to change in a luminous egg.

CHOICE-[CHOICE]: SEE: WARRIOR-CHOICE-[THE WARRIORS' CHOICE]

CLARITY-[CLARITY]: Warriors know that clarity is the property of mind that erases fear; this make-believe power of the warrior must be defied and used only to *see*; a point before the warriors' eyes and nothing more; the second natural enemy of the warrior.

CONTINUITY-[CONTINUITY]: Warriors know that continuity is the idea that we are a solid block; continuity is the underlying order of our self-reflection that sustains our world; the certainty that we are unchangeable; continuity is so important in the life of the average person that if it breaks, it's always repaired; once warriors' assemblage points reach the place of no pity, their continuity is never the same again; warriors must eventually create a new sense of continuity for themselves; they must become capable of intelligently utilizing their new continuity while invalidating the continuity of their old lives.

CONTRADICTION-KNOWLEDGE-[THE CONTRADICTIONS OF KNOWLEDGE]: SEE: WARRIOR-CONTRADICTION-KNOWLEDGE-[THE CONTRADICTIONS OF THE WARRIORS' QUEST FOR KNOWLEDGE]

CONTROL-WITHOUT-CONTROL-[CONTROL WITHOUT CONTROL]: Warriors know they must develop a way of being in control without controlling anything; the warriors' way of calculating their actions and then letting go once those calculations are over; the warriors' exercise of controlled abandon; the warriors' decisiveness in the face of power.

CONTROLLED-FOLLY[CONTROLLED FOLLY]: SEE: WARRIOR-CONTROLLED-FOLLY-[THE WARRIORS' CONTROLLED FOLLY]

CONTROLLED-FOLLY-ART-[THE ART OF CONTROLLED FOLLY]: Warriors know that the art of controlled folly is another term for the art of stalking.

CORE-GOOD-ROTTEN-[THE CORE OF EVERYTHING GOOD AND THE CORE OF EVERYTHING ROTTEN]: Warriors know that addressing the dilemma of everything good and rotten within themselves means addressing the dilemma of eliminating their own self-importance; self-importance is at the core of everything good and at the core of everything rotten in human beings; to eliminate the self-importance that is rotten while maintaining the good requires an impeccable masterpiece of strategy.

CREATIVE-ATTENTION-[CREATIVE ATTENTION]: Creative attention is the enhanced awareness of the practicing warrior-sorcerer.

CREATIVE-NAVIGATION-[CREATIVE NAVIGATION]: The guidance system used by warrior-sorcerers to direct their lives with their intuition and their intent.

CREATIVE-VICTORY-[CREATIVE VICTORY]: In the mysterious world of power, the warrior-sorcerers' creative victory must be redefined as the harmony of thought and action, the equanimity of the tonal and the nagual. *Creative victory* is a state of joyful balance and transcendence that emerges as we balance the *doing* and *not-doings* of warriorship and sorcery.

CREATIVITY-MOLDING-[MOLDING AND CREATIVITY]: Warriors know the difference between the pure creativity of the nagual and the superb molding abilities of the tonal; the nagual is the only part of the warrior that can create; the tonal cannot create anything, it can only witness and assess and mold things, personally or in conjunction with other tonals.

CYNICISM-[CYNICISM]: Warriors know the reason for mankind's cynicism and despair is the bit of silent knowledge left in us; this knowledge does two things; first, it gives mankind an inkling of the connection with intent, and second, it makes mankind feel that without this connection there is no hope for peace, satisfaction or attainment in life.

DAGGER-METAPHORICAL-[THE METAPHORICAL DAGGER]: Warriors know that average men and women share a metaphorical dagger, the concerns of their self-reflection; with this dagger they cut themselves and bleed, and it is the job of their self-reflection to make them feel as if they are bleeding together, sharing some sort of wonderful act of humanity; in reality though, they are not sharing anything, they are bleeding alone; when people cut themselves with this metaphorical dagger, they are only toying with their manageable but unreal, man-made reflection.

DEATH-ADVISER-[DEATH AS AN ADVISER]: Warriors know that it is the idea of death that tempers their spirit; death is the central force behind every bit of knowledge that becomes power; warriors consider themselves already dead, so they are clear and calm and without anything to lose; warriors have an awareness of the presence of death because without it there is no power, no mystery; the knowledge of death from which warriors draw the courage to face anything.

DEATH-CHOOSE-NOT-[WARRIORS DO NOT CHOOSE DEATH]: SEE: WARRIOR-DEATH-CHOOSE-NOT-[WARRIORS DO NOT CHOOSE DEATH]

DECISIONS-[DECISIONS]: SEE: WARRIOR-DECISIONS-[THE WARRIORS' DECISIONS]

DESCRIPTION-WORLD-[THE DESCRIPTION OF THE WORLD]: Warriors know that the description of the world is the "common sense" view of the world; a description, an interpretation of the world that our human senses make; the first attention's view of reality; the description of reason; the limited view of eternity that traps the totality of human beings in a vicious circle.

DESTINY-[DESTINY]: SEE: WARRIOR-DESTINY-[THE WARRIORS' DESTINY]

DETACHMENT-[DETACHMENT]: SEE: WARRIOR-DETACHMENT-[THE WARRIORS' DETACHMENT]

DIALOGUE-WARRIOR-[THE WARRIORS' DIALOGUE]: SEE: WARRIOR-DIALOGUE-[THE WARRIORS' DIALOGUE OF THE NEW SEERS]

DOING-[DOING]: Warriors know that a *doing* is something that contributes to making the world of solid objects; warriors know that an object is an object because we know how to *do* to it; this process is called *doing*.

DOOR-ONLY-[THE ONLY DOOR THERE IS]: Warriors know that the movement of the assemblage point beyond a certain limit results in the assemblage of other total worlds; the threshold of this critical movement is known as the only door there is.

DOUBT-POINT-NO-[THE POINT OF NO DOUBT]: Warriors know that the point of no doubt is a position of the assemblage point characterized by a peculiar feeling of having no doubts about things; a position of the assemblage point deeper into the left side from the position of normal awareness where the only thing one can *see* is blobs of energy; there are actually two points of no doubt for warriors; one is where they have no doubts because they know everything silently; the other is normal awareness where they have no doubts because they don't know anything.

DOUBTS-REMORSE-WARRIOR-[THE WARRIORS' DOUBTS AND REMORSE]: SEE: WARRIOR-DOUBTS-REMORSE-[THE WARRIORS' DOUBTS AND REMORSE]

DREAMING-ART-[THE ART OF DREAMING]: (Warriors know that the art of dreaming is the control of the natural shift that the assemblage point undergoes in sleep; the art of handling the dreaming body; the ultimate use of the nagual; the art of training the tonal to let go for a moment and then grab again; the art of dreaming is concerned with the movement or displacement of the assemblage point; one of the warriors' avenues to power; the art of transforming ordinary dreams into controlled awareness by virtue of the second attention; dreaming is the exercise of the second attention; the *not-doing* of sleep.

DREAMING-SETTING-UP-[SETTING UP DREAMING]: Warriors know they must develop a concise, pragmatic control over the general situation of a dream, comparable to the control one has while awake; the warriors' first step to power.

DROPPING-THINGS-LIVES-[DROPPING THINGS FROM OUR LIVES]: Warriors know that at any given moment they can drop anything from their lives that they choose, they can simply let things go.

EAGLE-[THE EAGLE]: Warriors know that the Eagle is the metaphorical name for the indescribable force that is the source of all sentient beings; the Eagle is the unknowable, a force that no human being can grasp; the power that governs the destiny of all living beings; the Eagle is not a literal eagle, nor does it have anything to do with a literal eagle; the Eagle only manifests itself to seers as something which resembles an eagle of infinite proportions; the Eagle bestows awareness on all living creatures and re-absorbs that same enriched awareness after making sentient beings relinquish it at the moment of death.

EAGLE-EMANATIONS-[THE EAGLE'S EMANATIONS]: Warriors know that the Eagle's emanations are an immutable thing that engulfs everything that exists, both knowable and unknowable; a presence, a mass of sorts, a pressure that creates a dazzling sensation; an indescribable presence that must be witnessed because there is no way to describe what it is; a brilliant array of live compelling fibers, each of which is an infinity unto itself; the fabric of the luminous universe; the energetic essence of everything; the essence of the universe; incandescent threads that are conscious of themselves in a way that is impossible for the human mind to comprehend.

EAGLE-GIFT-[THE EAGLE'S GIFT]: Warriors know that the Eagle's gift is an opportunity provided by the Eagle to all living beings, an opportunity to keep the flame of awareness; total freedom, total awareness is the Eagle's gift to mankind.

EARTH-[EARTH]: Warriors know the earth is an enormous sentient being; a lovely, nurturing being, alive to its last recesses; the earth understands, soothes and cures the warrior; the earth is a magnificent being that teaches warriors freedom and liberates their spirit.

EFFICIENCY-[EFFICIENCY]: SEE: WARRIOR-EFFICIENCY-[THE WARRIORS' EFFICIENCY]

EGO-[THE EGO]: Warriors know that there is no ego, there is only the tonal.

EGOMANIA-[EGOMANIA]: Warriors know that egomania is an expression of the first attention's sense of self.

EMPHASIS-[EMPHASIS]: SEE: WARRIOR-EMPHASIS-[THE WARRIORS' EMPHASIS]

EMPTINESS-[EMPTINESS]: SEE: WARRIOR-EMPTINESS-[THE WARRIORS' EMPTINESS]

ENEMIES-FOUR-NATURAL-WARRIOR-[THE FOUR NATURAL ENEMIES OF THE WARRIOR]: SEE: WARRIOR-ENEMIES-FOUR-NATURAL-[THE FOUR NATURAL ENEMIES OF THE WARRIOR]

ENERGY-[ENERGY]: Warriors know that energy is the luminous essence of mankind; one of the primary focuses of warriors is energy and the ability to save and rechannel it; the commodity that governs the warriors' ability to move the assemblage point and command the spirit; warriors must learn to re-deploy their energy in a more intelligent manner.

ENERGY-DRAINAGE-[PLUGGING POINTS OF ENERGY DRAINAGE]: Warriors know they must learn to store personal power by plugging up all their points of energy drainage; they don't have to be deliberate about it because power finds a way to accomplish this process; warriors assist the process by living the most impeccable life they possibly can even though power is unnoticeable to them as it is being stored; there is no more energy for warriors anywhere so they are forced to conserve the energetic resources that they already have.

ENLIGHTENMENT-[ENLIGHTENMENT]: Warriors know that enlightenment is the result of the true acquisition of knowledge, a process that occurs independent of language.

EQUAL-UNIMPORTANT-[EQUAL AND UNIMPORTANT]: Warriors who have learned to *see*, realize that everything is equal and unimportant.

EQUILIBRIUM-[EQUILIBRIUM]: Equilibrium is a mirror of the state of the warriors' totality, an impossible state of awareness that reflects the true balance of the energetic universe; at a given moment there is no longer a war within the warrior, because the warriors' way is harmony, first the harmony between actions and decisions and then the harmony between the tonal and the nagual.

ETERNITY-[ETERNITY]: Warriors define eternity as the immeasurable immensity that surrounds us; the third attention.

EVERYTHING-FILLED-BRIM-[EVERYTHING IS FILLED TO THE BRIM]: Warriors know that everything in their lives is equal and filled to the brim; there is no defeat or victory or emptiness, there is only the sense that everything is filled to the brim and that the warriors' struggle is worthwhile.

EXPECTATION-[EXPECTATION]: Warriors know it is stupidity that forces mankind to discard everything that does not conform to our self-reflective expectations.

EXPLANATION-[EXPLANATION]: Warriors know that explanations stem from the tonal's sterile and boring insistence on having everything under its control; warriors learn to do without explanations because the road to power is filled with things that are beyond words, things that can only be experienced or utilized; warriors know that explanations are never wasted because they are imprinted in us for immediate or later use or to help prepare the way to reach silent knowledge.

FACADE-TRANSFORMING-[TRANSFORMING THE FACADE]: Warriors know that transforming the facade refers to the sustained act of shifting the place of prominence of specific elements on the island of the tonal; warriors learn to emphasize the things that are truly important, like impeccability, and to de-emphasize those things that drain their power, like self-importance.

FATE-[FATE]: SEE: WARRIOR-FATE-[THE WARRIORS' FATE]

FINESSE-[FINESSE]: SEE: WARRIOR-FINESSE-[THE WARRIORS' FINESSE]

FIRE-WITHIN-[THE FIRE FROM WITHIN]: Warriors know that the fire from within is the force of the Eagle's emanations that enables warriors to burn with complete consciousness; the movement of the warriors' assemblage point across the entire field of luminous energy; the extension of the glow of awareness beyond the bounds of the luminous cocoon in one single stroke.

FLUIDITY-[FLUIDITY]: SEE: WARRIOR-FLUIDITY-[THE WARRIORS' FLUIDITY]

FORCE-CIRCULAR-[THE CIRCULAR FORCE]: Warriors know that the circular force is the life-giving aspect of the rolling force; the force that maintains life and awareness, fulfillment and purpose; the force of the emanations at large that acts as the incomprehensible life-giver and enhancer of awareness.

FORMLESSNESS-[FORMLESSNESS]: SEE: WARRIOR-FORMLESS-[FORMLESS WARRIORS]

FORMULA-[THE WARRIORS' FORMULA]: SEE: WARRIOR-FORMULA-[THE WARRIORS' FORMULA]

FREEDOM-TOTAL-[TOTAL FREEDOM]: Warriors know that their ultimate challenge is to dart past the Eagle and be free; the freedom of total awareness; a blast of unlimited consciousness; the Eagle's gift to mankind; total freedom means total awareness.

HABITS-UNNECESSARY-[UNNECESSARY HABITS]: (Warriors know they must maintain an objective perspective on their own habits and behavior as they relate to the quest for impeccability.

HARMONY-[HARMONY]: Warriors know that harmony is the balance of the warrior; the natural harmony of intent; at a given moment there is no longer a war within the warrior, because the warriors' way is harmony, first the harmony between actions and decisions and then the harmony between the tonal and the nagual; the harmony between actions and thought; the harmony between the tonal and the nagual.

HUMAN-ALTERNATIVES-POSSIBILITIES-POTENTIAL-[HUMAN ALTERNATIVES, POSSIBILITIES AND POTENTIAL]: Warriors know they must cultivate a comprehensive perspective on the limited alternatives presented to them by the first attention and the unlimited possibilities and potential of the second and third attentions; warriors struggle to extend themselves beyond the bounds of their first attention alternatives by discovering the unimaginable nature of their true potential.

HUMAN-FORM-[THE HUMAN FORM]: Warriors know that the human form is a force without form that makes human beings what they are; a force that possesses people all during their lives and normally doesn't leave them until the moment of death; normal human experience is all sifted through the human form; we act as humans because we cling to the human form; the compelling force of alignment of the emanations lit by the glow of awareness on the precise spot where the assemblage point is normally fixed.

HUMBLENESS-[HUMBLENESS]: SEE: WARRIOR-HUMBLENESS-[THE WARRIORS' HUMBLENESS]

IDIOCY-[IDIOCY]: Warriors know that many of the feelings of the average person are idiocy, and it takes all of the warriors' energy to conquer that idiocy within themselves.

IMPECCABILITY-STATE-OF-BEING-[AN IMPECCABLE STATE OF BEING]: Warriors know that seers who travel into the unknown to *see* the unknowable must be in an impeccable state of being; to be in an impeccable state of being is to be free from rational assumptions and rational fears.

INACCESSIBILITY-WARRIOR-[THE WARRIORS' INACCESSIBILITY]: SEE: WARRIOR-FOG-CREATE-[WARRIORS CREATE A FOG AROUND THEMSELVES]

INDOLENCE-[INDOLENCE, LAZINESS AND SELF-IMPORTANCE]: Warriors know that indolence, laziness and self-importance are all parts of the daily world; warriors struggle to overcome these aspects of the first attention that tend to muddle their aims, destroy their purpose, and make them weak.

INORGANIC-BEINGS-[THE INORGANIC BEINGS]: Warriors know that the inorganic beings are entities without organic life as we know it; formless energy fields; living creatures that are present on the earth and populate it together with organic beings.

INORGANIC-BEINGS-REALM-[THE REALM OF THE INORGANIC BEINGS]: Warriors know that in terms of the physicality of the universe, the realm of the inorganic beings exists in a particular position of the assemblage point, just as the everyday world exists in the habitual position of the assemblage point; the realm of the inorganic beings is the old sorcerers' field; in their own realm, the inorganic beings are as real as they can be, but in our world they are like moving pictures of rarefied energy projected through the boundaries of two worlds.

INTELLECT-DALLIANCE-[THE DALLIANCE OF THE INTELLECT]: Warriors know that it is always the intellect that fools warriors; instead of acting on things immediately, intellect always dallies with us instead.

IMPECCABILITY-[IMPECCABILITY]: SEE: WARRIOR-IMPECCABILITY-[THE WARRIORS' IMPECCABILITY]

INTENT-[INTENT]: Warriors know that intent is the abstract, the element that propels the warrior; intent is the flow of things, intent is the pervasive force that causes us to perceive; power; the force that permeates everything; intent is what makes the world.

INTENT-EDIFICE-[THE EDIFICE OF INTENT]: Warriors recognize the way intent causes things to happen around them; intent creates edifices and invites warriors to enter them.

INTENT-LINK-CLEANING-[CLEANING THE LINK WITH INTENT]:
Warriors know that the average person's link with intent has been numbed by the ordinary concerns of daily life; warriors strive to clean that link with intent by discussing, understanding and employing it; the connecting link of the average person is practically dead because it does not respond voluntarily; the warriors' path is a drastic process, the purpose of which is to bring the connecting link with intent to order; in order to revive the link with intent, warriors need a fierce purpose called unbending intent; the warriors' goal is to sensitize the connecting link with intent until it functions at will.

INTERVENTION-[INTERVENTION]: SEE: WARRIOR-INTERVENTION-[THE WARRIORS' INTERVENTION]

INTUITION-[INTUITION]: SEE: WARRIOR-INTUITION-[THE WARRIORS' INTUITION]

INVENTORY-[MANKIND'S INVENTORY]: Warriors know that the inventory is the mind of mankind; the inventory is the result of the way the first attention watches itself and takes notes about itself in whatever aberrant ways it can.

JOURNEY-DEFINITIVE-[THE WARRIORS' DEFINITIVE JOURNEY]: SEE: WARRIOR-JOURNEY-DEFINITIVE-[THE WARRIORS' DEFINITIVE JOURNEY]

JOURNEY-RETURN-[THE WARRIORS' JOURNEY OF RETURN]: SEE: WARRIOR-JOURNEY-RETURN-[THE WARRIORS' JOURNEY OF RETURN]

JOY-[JOY]: SEE: WARRIOR-JOY-[THE WARRIORS' JOY]

JUAN-MATUS-[DON JUAN MATUS]: A Yaqui Indian warrior-sorcerer-seer who was the teacher of Carlos Castaneda.

KINDNESS-[KINDNESS]: Warriors know that kindness is one name for the bridge between contradictions; the counterpoint to wisdom; that which makes wisdom useful and meaningful.

KNOWLEDGE-[KNOWLEDGE]: Warriors think of knowledge as the knowledge of nagualism; also referred to as the mastery of intent, the search for total freedom, or sorcery.

KNOWLEDGE-ABSTRACT-[THE ABSTRACT ORDER OF KNOWLEDGE]: Warriors know that the abstract order of knowledge is the underlying order of nagualism, the edifice that intent places in front of warriors and the signs that it gives them so they won't get lost once they are inside; the ulterior arrangement of the abstract; silent knowledge.

KNOWLEDGE-ACCEPTING-PROPOSITIONS-[ACCEPTING THE PROPOSITIONS OF KNOWLEDGE]: Warriors know that actually accepting the propositions of knowledge is not as easy as saying one accepts them; the crux of mankind's difficulty in returning to the abstract is our refusal to accept that knowledge can exist independent of language or thoughts.

KNOWLEDGE-AVAILABILITY-[THE AVAILABILITY OF KNOWLEDGE]: Warriors know that knowledge remains unavailable to them until their energy level comes on par with the importance of what they know; energy tends to be cumulative, and if warriors follow an impeccable path, a moment will come one day when their memories will open up.

KNOWLEDGE-CLAIMING-POWER-[CLAIMING KNOWLEDGE AS POWER]: Warriors know that they must claim knowledge as part of a personal internalization process; warriors know that they must accumulate personal power in order to claim their knowledge; this process applies to both the tonal and the nagual; warriors must claim informational knowledge through reason and claim the knowledge of mysteries by doing that which they have been shown.

KNOWLEDGE-VS-LANGUAGE-[KNOWLEDGE VS LANGUAGE]: Warriors know that knowledge exists independent of language or information; there is no way to talk about the abstract, the abstract can only be experienced; the deeper the assemblage point moves, the greater the feeling that warriors have knowledge and no words to explain it.

KNOWLEDGE-MAN-[MANKIND'S KNOWLEDGE]: Warriors know that when mankind became aware of silent knowledge and we wanted to be conscious of what we knew, we lost sight of what we knew; the error of the human race was to want to know silent knowledge directly, the way we know everyday life; the more mankind tried to know silent knowledge, the more ephemeral it became; in the end mankind gave up silent knowledge for the world of reason.

KNOWLEDGE-PATH-[THE PATH OF KNOWLEDGE]: Warriors know that the path to knowledge is the road to total awareness; a forced path, a path on which warriors are always fighting something, avoiding something or preparing for something that is inexplicable and greater than themselves; the warriors' journey with power, a path on which only impeccability matters; a path that leads warriors to their own hidden power.

KNOWLEDGE-SILENT-[SILENT KNOWLEDGE]: Warriors know that silent knowledge is a position of the assemblage point; the warriors' direct knowledge; the knowledge of the body; *seeing*.

KNOWN-[KNOWN]: Warriors know that the known is the minute fraction of the Eagle's emanations within the reach of normal human awareness; the first attention; right side awareness; the attention of the tonal.

LEARNING-[LEARNING]: Warriors know that learning is their lot in life, to learn and to be hurled into inconceivable new worlds; the warriors' sincere desire to learn.

LETTING-GO-[LETTING GO]: Warriors know they must learn to act with abandon, to let go of their first attention agendas and inventory; the gentle art of letting go; the warriors' ability to let go of the desire to cling to things, people, self-reflection and other specifics of the world of solid objects.

LIENS-MORTGAGES-[LIENS AND MORTGAGES]: Warriors know that their liens and mortgages are the edifices of morbidity, obsession and self-importance; the things that weigh heavily on warriors and impede their progress on the path of knowledge.

LIFE-MODERN-TURNING-AWAY-[TURNING AWAY FROM MODERN LIFE]: Warriors know that mankind has exchanged the realm of the mysterious for the realm of the functional; warriors live in the midst of the modern world but turn their backs away from the focus of modern society; warriors embrace the world of mystery and foreboding in favor of the world of boredom.

LIGHTNESS-[LIGHTNESS]: SEE: WARRIOR-LIGHTNESS-[THE WARRIORS' LIGHTNESS]

LINES-WORLD-[THE LINES OF THE WORLD]: Warriors know that the lines of the world are a visual manifestation of the Eagle's emanations that warriors can "hook" themselves on to and utilize to move their bodies.

LOOKING-VS-SEEING-[LOOKING VS SEEING]: Warriors know about the distinctions between the two separate manners of perceiving; "looking" refers to the way we normally perceive the world of solid objects through the eyes of the first attention; *"seeing"* refers to the way warriors perceive the world with their entire bodies and are able to view the luminous essence of the world instead; "looking" involves viewing the tonal that is in everything; *"seeing"* involves viewing the nagual that is in everything.

LOVE-[LOVE]: SEE: WARRIOR-LOVE-[THE WARRIORS' LOVE]

LUMINOUS-BEINGS-[LUMINOUS BEINGS]: Warriors know that all organic and inorganic life forms are luminous beings.

LUMINOUS-BUBBLE-[THE LUMINOUS BUBBLE]: Warriors know that human beings are made of the Eagle's emanations and are, in essence, bubbles of luminescent energy, wrapped in a cocoon that encloses a small portion of those emanations.

LUMINOUS-COCOON-[THE LUMINOUS COCOON]: Warriors know that the luminous cocoon is a transparent structure shared by human beings and all sentient beings; the configurations of these cocoons vary, but all sentient beings are alike insofar as their emanations are encased inside some kind of luminous cocoon; the luminous shell.

MAGIC-[MAGIC]: Warriors know that magic is the true heritage of mankind; magic can be described as the simple act of awareness, the ability of human beings to keep the assemblage point fixed; the ability of human beings to impart order to that which they perceive; the force that fills warriors and banishes doubt from their minds.

MAN-DEPENDENT-[MANKIND IS DEPENDENT]: Warriors know that human beings are dependent; we crave someone to guide us when in reality, nothing stops us from accomplishing everything by ourselves; we are unwilling to accept that we need so little to get on with the most essential work of our lives.

MAN-DESPAIR-[MANKIND'S DESPAIR]: Warriors know that man's despair springs from the bit of silent knowledge left in us that does two things; first that knowledge gives us an inkling of our ancient connection with intent; second, it makes us feel that without that connection we will find no peace, no satisfaction, and no attainment.

MAN-EVOLUTION-[MANKIND IS CAPABLE OF EVOLVING]: Warriors know that mankind is capable of evolving; in order to do so, we must free our awareness from the bindings of the social order; once our awareness is free, intent will redirect it onto a new evolutionary path; sorcerers are the proof that this evolution is possible.

MAN-FALLACY-[THE FALLACY OF MANKIND]: Warriors know that the average person is inclined to totally disregard the link with intent and the magic of existence; average people believe in their madness that they are all tonal, and totally disregard the nagual.

MAN-MALADY-[THE MALADY OF MANKIND]: Warriors know that mankind's malady is that we know infinitely more about the mystery of the universe than we rationally suspect.

MAN-MISERY-[THE SOURCE OF MANKIND'S MISERY]: Warriors know that self-pity is their true enemy and the source of man's misery; self-pity leads to self-importance which in turn develops its own momentum and gives rise to man's fake sense of worth.

MAN-NEEDS-[WHAT MANKIND NEEDS NOW]: Warriors know that what mankind needs now is be taught ideas pertaining to facing the unknown; human beings need to be taught ideas that will pull them away from the outer world and reconnect them with the inner world of the abstract; human beings need to be taught the secrets of the assemblage point; human beings need to be taught how to abstract themselves; what we need is to allow magic to get hold of us and banish all doubt from our minds; once those doubts have been erased, anything is possible; human beings need help in reconnecting with the abstract, not through methods, but through emphasis; if someone makes a human being aware of the need to curtail self-importance, then that help is real.

MAN-PLIGHT-[MANKIND'S PLIGHT]: Warriors know that mankind's plight is the counterpoint between our stupidity and our ignorance.

MAN-SPIRIT-ACCOUNT-[PAYING BACK TO THE ACCOUNT OF THE SPIRIT OF MANKIND]: Warriors make deposits to the account of the spirit of mankind as their way of repaying the kindness and generosity of others they have encountered on their path; the account of the spirit of mankind is very small, but any impeccable deposit one makes is always more than enough.

MIND-[THE MIND]: Warriors know that the mind is nothing more than the self-reflection of the inventory of mankind; the mind is our rationality, and our rationality is our self-reflection.

MINIMAL-CHANCE-[THE MINIMAL CHANCE]: SEE: WARRIOR-CHANCE-MINIMAL-[THE WARRIORS' MINIMAL CHANCE]:

MIRACLE-[MIRACLE]: Warriors know that a miracle is a manifestation of the nagual; a manifestation of the spirit perceived in conjunction with a movement of the assemblage point; when the tonal shrinks, extraordinary things are possible, but these miracles are only extraordinary for the tonal.

MORBIDITY-[MORBIDITY]: SEE: ABERRATION-MORBIDITY-[ABERRATION AND MORBIDITY]

NAGUAL-[THE NAGUAL]: Warriors know that the nagual, pronounced (nah-wa'hl), is the abstract, intent, the indescribable, the second attention, power, the spirit.

NAGUALISM-[NAGUALISM]: Warriors know that nagualism is the most appropriate name for the warrior-sorcerer's knowledge.

NOT-DOING-[NOT-DOING]: Warriors know that *not-doing* is any unfamiliar act that engages our total being by forcing it to become conscious of its luminous segment; the opposite of *doing*.

NOTHING-EVERYTHING-[NOTHING AND EVERYTHING]: Warriors know that when they experience *seeing*, everything becomes nothing; everything is here and yet it isn't here at all; warriors prepare themselves to be aware, and full awareness comes only when there is no more self-importance left in them; only when warriors are nothing can they hope to become everything.

OMEN-[OMENS]: Warriors know that omens are acts of power, indications of the spirit; the cubic centimeter of chance; manifestations of the spirit; gestures of the spirit; the edifice of intent.

PAIR-TRUE-[THE TRUE PAIR]: Warriors know that the tonal and the nagual are the members of the one true pair; the two components of the warriors' totality.

PATH-HEART-WITH-[THE PATH WITH HEART]: For warriors there is only traveling on paths with heart; the path with heart makes for a joyful journey; as long as warriors follow their path with heart, they are one with it.

PEACE-[PEACE]: SEE: WARRIOR-PEACE-[PEACE FOR THE WARRIOR]

PERCEPTION-[PERCEPTION]: Warriors know that perception takes place when the Eagle's emanations inside the luminous cocoon align themselves with the corresponding emanations at large; perception takes place because the assemblage point selects internal and external emanations for alignment; perception occurs when the Eagle's emanations in the small group immediately surrounding the assemblage point extend their light to illuminate identical emanations outside the luminous cocoon.

PERCEPTION-BARRIER-BREAKING-[BREAKING THE BARRIER OF PERCEPTION]: Warriors know that when the assemblage point moves away from its customary position to a certain degree, it breaks a barrier that momentarily disrupts its capacity to align emanations; this threshold is experienced as a moment of perceptual blankness; breaking the barrier of perception is the culmination of everything that warriors do, and it confirms their ability to move the assemblage point to the degree necessary to actually assemble other worlds.

PERCEPTION-CHANGING-SOCIAL-BASE-[CHANGING THE SOCIAL BASE OF PERCEPTION]: Warriors know it is necessary for mankind to learn to separate the social part of our perception; we must learn to modify the foundation of our perception from a base of concreteness to a basis predicated on the abstract; the social base of our perception should be the physical certainty that energy is all there is.

PITY-PLACE-NO-[THE PLACE OF NO PITY]: Warriors know that the place of no pity is a specific position of the assemblage point that shines in the eyes of sorcerers; the site of ruthlessness.

POINT-THIRD-[THE THIRD POINT, THE THIRD POINT OF REFERENCE]: Warriors know that the third point is another term for silent knowledge.

POINT-THIRD-INVERSION-[THE INVERSION OF THE THIRD POINT]: Warriors know that the third point became inverted at some point in mankind's ancient past; reason, which is now the first point, used to be the third point and silent knowledge, which used to be the first point, is now the third point.

POWER-[POWER]: Warriors know power is something they simply deal with; an incredible far-fetched affair; power is a feeling one has about certain things; power commands warriors and yet it obeys them.

POWER-ACTS-[ACTS OF POWER]: Warriors know that acts of power are expressions of the nagual; expressions of the warriors' intent.

POWER-AVENUES-[THE AVENUES TO POWER]: Warriors know that power provides avenues to us in accordance with our impeccability.

POWER-DESIGNS-[THE DESIGNS OF POWER]: Warriors know that they must humbly accept the nature and designs of power; warriors understand that no one can discern the designs of power, because the spirit always decides its own course; power is and power moves, these are the only things that warriors know for sure.

POWER-FLOW-[THE FLOW OF POWER]: Warriors know they can never guess or determine how power will flow to them; no person can say that power would have flowed to them if their life would have been different.

POWER-HIDDEN-[MANKIND'S HIDDEN POWER]: Warriors know that power is accessible to every human being at all times; the warriors' path of knowledge really involves nothing more than allowing ourselves to be convinced that power is hidden in our being and that it is possible for us to access it.

POWER-IS-POWER-MOVES-[POWER IS AND POWER MOVES]: Warriors know that there is no explanation for the fact that power exists and that it moves inexplicably and of its own accord.

POWER-OBJECT-[POWER OBJECTS]: Warriors know that certain objects are permeated with power; the nature of these objects is to be at war, because the part of our attention that focuses on them to give them power is a very dangerous and belligerent part of ourselves.

POWER-PERSONAL-[PERSONAL POWER]: Warriors know that personal power is like a mood or a feeling, something like being lucky; warriors store personal power by living and acting impeccably; warriors understand that they are only the sum of their personal power.

POWER-PREAMBLE-[THE PREAMBLE OF POWER]: The Toltec path of knowledge begins with the intervention of intent, a revelation that opens the existence of power's promise to the heart and mind of a given individual. Under the appropriate circumstances, this manifestation of the spirit leads to the internalization of a series of ultra personal insights regarding the nature of the energetic universe and the essential and incomprehensible relationship between the luminous beings and power itself. The assimilation of these critical insights is known as the preamble of power.

POWER-PROCESS-[THE PROCESS OF POWER]: The process of power is the incomprehensible dynamic that moves human beings through the portal of power with their entire bodies. This process is characterized by the movement of the assemblage point from the position of normal awareness to the position of total awareness.

POWER-PROMISE-[THE PROMISE OF POWER]: Warriors know that the promise of power is the fulfillment of the designs of power for the warrior; the promise of power is a promise that power makes to all men and women as luminous beings; every warrior has a different fate and there is no way of telling what the promise of power will be for any given individual; the promise of power can be summarized as follows: "One day each and every human being will return to the abstract in a state of total awareness."

POWER-RING-FIRST-[THE FIRST RING OF POWER]: Warriors know that the first ring of power is the little ring of power, the ring of power that is hooked to the *doing* of the world.

POWER-RING-SECOND-[THE SECOND RING OF POWER]: Warriors know that the second ring of power is the ring of power developed by a "man or woman of knowledge", the ring of *not-doing*.

POWER-TALES-[TALES OF POWER]: For the warrior apprentice there is only witnessing acts of power and listening to tales of power; tales of power are also known as sorcery stories.

PREDILECTION-[THE WARRIORS' PREDILECTION]: SEE: WARRIOR-PREDILECTION-[THE WARRIORS' PREDILECTION]

PROACTIVITY-[PROACTIVITY]: SEE: WARRIOR-PROACTIVITY-[THE WARRIORS' PROACTIVITY]

REALIZATION-[REALIZATION]: Warriors know there are two kinds of realizations; one is just a pep talk, a great outburst of emotion and nothing more; the other is a product of a shift of the assemblage point that is not coupled with an emotional outburst but with action; warriors place the highest value on deep, unemotional realizations.

REASON-[REASON AND RATIONALITY]: Warriors know that reason or rationality is a condition of alignment, merely a by-product of the habitual position of the assemblage point; the first ring of power.

REASON-CLINGING-[CLINGING TO REASON]: Warriors know they must struggle to convince their reason, their tonal, to become free and fluid; warriors know that the more they cling to the world of reason, the more ephemeral intent becomes.

REASON-VANQUISHING-[VANQUISHING REASON]: Warriors know they must struggle to suppress or "vanquish" the attention of the tonal, not reason or the capacity for rational thought per se.

RECAPITULATION-[RECAPITULATION]: Warriors know that the recapitulation is the forte of stalkers as the dreaming body is the forte of dreamers; the task of recapitulation consists of recollecting one's own life down to the most insignificant detail.

REMORSE-DOUBTS-[DOUBTS AND REMORSE]: SEE: WARRIOR-DOUBTS-REMORSE-[THE WARRIORS' DOUBTS AND REMORSE]

RESPONSIBILITY-ASSUMING-[ASSUMING RESPONSIBILITY]: Warriors know they must take full responsibility for each and every one of their actions; no matter what they do, they must first know why they are acting, and then they must proceed with their actions without having doubts or remorse about them.

REST-[REST]: Another term for impeccability, the action of rechanneling energy in the most strategic way possible; rest is the essence of warrior-ship, or the way of the impeccable action.

RULE-[THE RULE]: Warriors know that the rule is an absolute truth; an endless map to the universe which covers every aspect of the warriors' behavior; being involved with the rule may be described as living a myth; the warrior at first conceptualizes the rule as a myth and later comes to understand it and accept it as a map.

RUTHLESSNESS-[RUTHLESSNESS]: Warriors know that ruthlessness is the first principle of sorcery; the place of no pity is the site of ruthlessness; ruthlessness is a specific position of the assemblage point that shines in the eyes of sorcerers; ruthlessness is sobriety, it should not be harshness.

SCALES-TIP-[TIP THE SCALES]: Warriors know the term "tip the scales" refers to a level of personal power that makes it possible for them to cross a threshold of awareness through a shift or movement of the assemblage point.

SCHOLAR-WORLD-ARRANGEMENT-[THE SCHOLAR'S ARRANGEMENT OF THE WORLD]: Warriors know that scholars arrange the world in a beautiful and enlightened manner from 8:00 A.M. to 5:00 P.M. and then go home in order to forget about their beautiful arrangement; the scholar's arrangement of the world is inadequate because words themselves are inadequate; warriors know that true knowledge is independent of language altogether.

SEEING-[SEEING]: Warriors know that *seeing* is another term for moving the assemblage point; *seeing* is a way of witnessing the world with one's entire body; *seeing* is to lay bare the core of everything, to witness the unknown and to glimpse into the unknowable.

SEER-NEW-[THE NEW SEERS]: Warriors know that the new seers are the seers of the new cycle; "los nuevos videntes"; modern day sorcerers; the new seers are terribly practical men and women, they aren't involved in concocting rational theories; the new seers have corrected the mistakes of the old seers by applying what they've learned through *seeing*.

SEER-OLD-[THE OLD SEERS]: Warriors know that the old seers are the ancient seers of the old cycle, the sorcerers of antiquity; most of the fundamental knowledge of the new seers was figured out by the old seers; the knowledge of the old seers led them to total destruction, so the new seers had to reevaluate the procedures of their immense tradition and sort out the errors the old seers had made; the old seers were masters of conjecture, they made several critical assumptions that led them to a most precarious position with regard to the unknown and the unknowable; the old seers became aberrant and morbidly obsessed; their bid is to dominate, to master everybody and everything.

SELF-[THE SELF]: Warriors know that ancient members of the human race knew, in the most direct fashion, what to do and how to do it; but because we performed so well, we began to develop a feeling of "selfness" which gave us the feeling that we could predict and plan the actions we were used to performing, and thus the idea of an individual self appeared; this individual sense of self began to dictate the nature and scope of mankind's actions; warriors battle to detach themselves from the individual self that has deprived them of their power; the self is the sense of individual existence.

SELF-COMPASSION-[SELF-COMPASSION]: Warriors know self-compassion is a by-product of self-importance; self-compassion is self-pity in disguise; the position of self-reflection forces the assemblage point to assemble a world of sham compassion, but very real cruelty and self-centeredness.

SELF-DESTRUCTION-[SELF-DESTRUCTION]: Warriors know that modern human beings have become hopelessly removed from intent and all we can do is express our despair in violent and cynical acts of self-destruction.

SELF-IMAGE-[THE SELF-IMAGE]: Warriors know that the average person is totally involved with their self-image; the self-image cannot be sustained once the assemblage point moves past a particular threshold; the human being who holds fast to their self-image insures their abysmal ignorance by doing so.

SELF-IMPORTANCE-[SELF-IMPORTANCE]: Warriors know that self-importance is the force generated by mankind's self-image; it is the force that keeps the assemblage point fixed at its habitual position.

SELF-IMPORTANCE-LOSING-[LOSING SELF-IMPORTANCE]: The thrust of the warriors' way is to dethrone self-importance; warriors cannot believe that they are above anyone because they know that they are really nothing; warriors cannot travel into the non-human unknown until they have completely lost their self-importance; if warriors need help it is not with methods but with emphasis, and if someone makes them aware of the need to curtail self-importance, that help is real.

SELF-IMPORTANCE-MONSTER-THREE-THOUSAND-HEADS-[THE MONSTER OF SELF-IMPORTANCE WITH THREE THOUSAND HEADS]: Warriors know that self-importance can be described as a monster with three thousand heads.

SELF-INDULGENCE-[SELF-INDULGENCE]: Warriors know that indulging is another name for the way the average person weakens their tonal; warriors refuse to weaken themselves in this way, and instead accept in humbleness what they are; taking the easy way out is the indulging way, not the warriors' way.

SELFISHNESS-[SELFISHNESS]: Warriors know they must seek to harness the power of selfishness by turning it around and putting it to good use; the surest way of accomplishing that is through the daily activity of life.

SELF-PITY-[SELF-PITY]: Warriors know that self-pity is the real enemy and the source of mankind's misery; self-importance springs from a degree of pity for oneself.

SELF-REFLECTION-[SELF-REFLECTION]: Warriors know the position of self-reflection is the mind of mankind, the self-reflection of the inventory; self-reflection is a position of the assemblage point.

SKIMMINGS-[SKIMMINGS]: Warriors know that skimmings are a tricky refinement of perception; a human construct with no parallel; the skimmings of mankind represent the further clustering of the clusters of the Eagle's emanations; mankind's assemblage point takes some part of the emanations already selected for alignment and makes an even more palatable construct with them; the skimmings of mankind are more "real" than what other creatures perceive, and to give those skimmings a free hand is an error in judgment for which we pay dearly; it is our pitfall to forget that our skimmings are real only because it is our command to perceive them as real.

SOBRIETY-[SOBRIETY]: SEE: WARRIOR-SOBRIETY-[THE WARRIORS' SOBRIETY]

SOLIDITY-[SOLIDITY]: SEE: WARRIOR-SOLIDITY-[THE WARRIORS' SOLIDITY]

SORCERER-ABSTRACT-[THE TRUE ABSTRACT SORCERER]: The warrior-sorcerer is defined as a true abstract sorcerer; instead of merely being part of a morbid and ignorant audience of lovers of the unknown, true warrior-sorcerers have abstracted themselves.

SORCERER-ANTIQUITY-[THE SORCERERS OF ANTIQUITY]: Warriors know that the sorcerers of antiquity is another term for the old seers; the ancient Toltecs.

SORCERY-[SORCERY]: Warriors know that sorcery is the application of knowledge and power by the individual; sorcery is a state of awareness; sorcery is the attempt to reestablish our knowledge of intent, the act of reaching the place of silent knowledge.

SPIRIT-[SPIRIT]: Warriors know the spirit is the abstract, the spirit is intent; the spirit is something with no parallel in the human condition; the spirit is the force that sustains the universe; the spirit is not an entity or a presence; power; the spirit has no essence and yet it can be beckoned and enticed to come forward.

SPIRIT-DESCENT-[THE DESCENT OF THE SPIRIT]: Warriors know that the fourth abstract core is the descent of the spirit or the act of the spirit revealing itself to the warrior; sorcerers describe it as the spirit lying in ambush for us and then descending on us, its prey; the spirit's descent is always shrouded, it happens but it seems not to have happened at all.

SPIRIT-DESIGNS-[THE DESIGNS OF THE SPIRIT]: Warriors know they must move through life watching for the designs of the spirit to reveal themselves; instead of allowing pettiness to choose all the things in their lives, they become silent and proceed as the spirit directs them to proceed.

SPIRIT-MANIFESTATIONS-[MANIFESTATIONS OF THE SPIRIT]: Warriors know that the manifestations of the spirit is another term for omens; the spirit tends to keep its distance until something entices it forward; it is then that the spirit manifests itself.

STALKER-BREATH-[THE STALKERS' BREATH]: Warriors know that the stalkers' breath is the key element in the warriors' recapitulation; breath is a magical, life-giving function that restores the luminosity of the warrior.

STALKING-ART-[THE ART OF STALKING]: Warriors know that the art of stalking is a set of procedures and attitudes that enable us to get the most out of any conceivable situation.

STRATEGY-[STRATEGY]: SEE: WARRIOR-STRATEGY-[THE WARRIORS' STRATEGY]

STUPIDITY-IGNORANCE-[STUPIDITY AND IGNORANCE]: Warriors know that mankind's plight is the counterpoint between our stupidity and our ignorance; warriors act to demean the stupidity of mankind by understanding it and taking steps to surmount it through the way of the impeccable action.

THINKING-[THINKING]: Warriors know the limitations of their thinking; warriors knows that the mysterious world does not always conform to their thoughts.

TOLTEC-[TOLTECS]: Warriors know that Toltec means "man or woman of knowledge"; the Toltecs were ancient sorcerer-seers, the receivers and holders of mysteries; when warriors receive the mysteries of stalking and dreaming they become Toltecs.

TONAL-[THE TONAL]: Warriors know that the tonal, pronounced (toh-na'hl), is the organizer of the world; the tonal is everything we know, everything in our world, everything that meets the eye.

TONAL-ISLAND-[THE ISLAND OF THE TONAL]: Warriors know that the tonal is an island, an island on which we have everything; an island which is in fact, the world; warriors never leave the island of the tonal, they use it instead; the only alternative warriors have is to sweep clean the island of the tonal.

TONAL-SUICIDE-[THE SUICIDAL TENDENCIES OF THE TONAL]: Warriors know that the tonal has a sterile and boring insistence on having everything under its control; whenever it doesn't succeed, there is a moment of bafflement when the tonal opens itself to death; in some way the tonal would rather kill itself than relinquish control and there is very little warriors can do to change that condition.

UNKNOWABLE-[THE UNKNOWABLE]: Warriors know that the unknowable is the indescribable, the unthinkable, the unrealizable.

UNKNOWN-[THE UNKNOWN]: Warriors know that the unknown and the known are on the same footing because both are within the reach of human perception; the small portion of the Eagle's emanations within the reach of human awareness is the unknown; at a given time in the lives of warrior-sorcerers, the unknown becomes the known; warriors also understand the critical difference between the unknown and the unknowable.

VICTIM-[VICTIM]: Warriors know that average people remain victims because they believe they are helpless like leaves in the wind; warriors, however, assume responsibility for themselves, because they know that nobody is doing anything to anybody, much less to a warrior.

VICTORY-[VICTORY]: Warriors know they are in the hands of power and there is no way to fake triumph or defeat; warriors do not win victories by beating their heads against walls but by overtaking those walls instead; sorcery is a journey of return and warriors return victorious to the spirit having descended into hell; the victories of the warrior are victories of the spirit.

VICTORY-DEFEAT-EQUAL-[VICTORY AND DEFEAT ARE EQUAL]: Warriors know that victory and defeat are equal because everything in the world of the tonal is equal and unimportant; the spirit of warriors is geared only for struggle and the outcome of our struggle is relatively unimportant.

VOLUNTEERS-[VOLUNTEERS]: Warriors know that volunteers are not welcome in the sorcerers' world because they have a purpose of their own which makes it hard for them to relinquish their individual selves.

WAR-WARRIOR-[WAR FOR THE WARRIOR]: SEE WARRIOR-WAR-[WAR FOR THE WARRIOR]

WARRIOR-[THE WARRIOR]: One who has been led by power to an apprenticeship in the warriors' way; it is an honor and a pleasure to be a warrior and it is the fortune of warriors to do what they must do; warriors are true thinkers and abstract sorcerers; warriors are human beings in direct contact with the spirit.

WARRIOR-ACQUIESCENCE-[THE WARRIORS' ACQUIESCENCE]: Warriors know the true nature of their decisions; warriors acknowledge that something beyond their understanding has set up the framework of their so-called decisions, and all warriors do is acquiesce to it; warriors acquiesce to their fate, not passively like idiots, but actively like warriors.

WARRIOR-AIRBORNE-[AIRBORNE WARRIORS]: For warriors, dreaming and recapitulating go hand in hand; as warriors regurgitate their lives, they become more and more airborne.

WARRIOR-ARTS-[THE WARRIORS' ARTS]: The many arts of the warrior; activities that warriors perform as part of the warriors' way; dreaming, stalking, controlled folly and balancing the tonal against the nagual are among the warriors' performing arts.

WARRIOR-BRIDGE-[THE WARRIORS' BRIDGE]: The warriors' bridge is the invisible span between the contradictory propositions of knowledge.

WARRIOR-CARING-FOR-ANOTHER-[CARING FOR ANOTHER WARRIOR]: Warriors know that sometimes part of their task is to look after another warrior; warriors consider it an honor to look after another warrior in this way; warriors harness their selfishness by extending their selfish concern to include another.

WARRIOR-CHANCE-MINIMAL-[THE WARRIORS' MINIMAL CHANCE]: The warriors' minimal chance is the magical opportunity that power provides for warriors; the cubic centimeter of chance that pops out in front of the warriors' eyes from time to time; the gesture of the spirit; the warriors' minimal chance is not instruction, but rather the chance to become aware of the spirit.

WARRIOR-CHOICE-[THE WARRIORS' CHOICE]: Warriors know that at a specific point during their apprenticeship, they must make a critical choice; they either choose the warriors' world or choose the world of the average person; in the end warriors realize that this critical choice never really exists, because they have no real choice, they are in the hands of power.

WARRIOR-CONTRADICTION-KNOWLEDGE-[THE CONTRADICTIONS OF THE WARRIORS' QUEST FOR KNOWLEDGE]: Warriors know that the road to knowledge is filled with contradictory propositions; warriors struggle to pit two views of the world against each other, and in the process, somehow manage to wriggle between them to find the totality of themselves; the warriors' awareness that knowledge is composed of a set of contradictory propositions.

WARRIOR-CONTROLLED-FOLLY-[THE WARRIORS' CONTROLLED FOLLY]: Warriors know that controlled folly is the art of controlled deception, or the art of pretending to be thoroughly immersed in the action at hand; controlled folly is a sophisticated, artistic way of being separated from everything while remaining an integral part of everything.

WARRIOR-DEATH-CHOOSE-NOT-[WARRIORS DO NOT CHOOSE DEATH]: Warriors know they must choose life, not death; warriors prepare themselves to be aware and they know that to seek death is to seek nothing.

WARRIOR-DECISIONS-[THE WARRIORS' DECISIONS]: Warriors know they must learn to empower their ability to decide and to be decisive; warriors know that deciding doesn't mean choosing an arbitrary time; deciding means that warriors have trimmed their spirit impeccably and have done everything possible to be worthy of knowledge and power.

WARRIOR-DESTINY-[THE WARRIORS' DESTINY]: Warriors know that there is no destiny, only the fulfillment of power's promise.

WARRIOR-DETACHMENT-[THE WARRIORS' DETACHMENT]: Warriors struggle to detach themselves from everything; the detachment of the warrior is not born out of fear or indolence, but out of conviction.

WARRIOR-DIALOGUE-[THE WARRIORS' DIALOGUE OF THE NEW SEERS]: Warriors carry on a dialogue to help solidify the new position of their assemblage point; warriors know that the dialogue of the new seers is really not a dialogue at all but the detached manipulation of intent through sober commands; warriors feel a compelling desire to explain sorcery in cogent, well-reasoned terms, and they utilize this desire as an intellectual exercise with which to stalk themselves.

WARRIOR-DOUBTS-REMORSE-[THE WARRIORS' DOUBTS AND REMORSE]: Warriors must assume full responsibility for what they do; they must be clear as to why they act and then proceed with their actions without doubts or remorse; acting without doubts and remorse is the only way warriors can empower their decisions.

WARRIOR-EFFICIENCY-[THE WARRIORS' EFFICIENCY]: Warriors strive to strike a subtle balance of positive and negative forces which will enable them to meet any conceivable situation with equal efficiency.

WARRIOR-EMPHASIS-[THE WARRIORS' EMPHASIS]: The warriors' emphasis is the way warriors prioritize the items on the island of the tonal; the key to the warriors' choices; warriors can make themselves miserable or they can make themselves strong; either way the amount of work is the same, so the key lies in what one emphasizes; if warriors can benefit from anything, it is not from methods but from a change of emphasis.

WARRIOR-EMPTINESS-[THE WARRIORS' EMPTINESS]: The warriors' emptiness is written on the luminous body, it is a hole or series of holes in the luminous cocoon; the act of having children empties warriors and makes them incomplete.

WARRIOR-ENEMIES-FOUR-NATURAL-[THE FOUR NATURAL ENEMIES OF THE WARRIOR]: Warriors know they have a series of four natural enemies that they must face and conquer on the road to knowledge; the four enemies of the warrior are fear, clarity, power and old age.

WARRIOR-FATE-[THE WARRIORS' FATE]: Warriors give themselves to the power that rules their fate; warriors acquiesce to their fate, not passively like idiots, but actively like warriors; warriors know that it does not matter what their fate is, as long as they face it with ultimate abandon.

WARRIOR-FINESSE-[THE WARRIORS' FINESSE]: Warriors always act with the utmost finesse because they are aware that the worst thing one can do is to confront human beings bluntly; the warriors' reasons are simple, but their finesse is extreme.

WARRIOR-FLUIDITY-[THE WARRIORS' FLUIDITY]: Warriors are trained to be fluid, to be at ease in whatever situation they find themselves; when warriors burn with the fire from within they become fluid in the ultimate sense, they become what they really are, fluid, forever in motion, eternal; the warriors' fluidity enables them to glide effortlessly from the most sublime situations to the most ludicrous.

WARRIOR-FORMLESS-[FORMLESS WARRIORS]: The warriors' formlessness is the condition of having lost the human form; when warriors have no form then nothing has form and yet everything is present.

WARRIOR-FORMULA-[THE WARRIORS' FORMULA]: The warriors' formula is an affirmation of the warriors' reality; "I am already given to the power that rules my fate. And I cling to nothing, so I will have nothing to defend. I have no thoughts so I will *see*. I fear nothing so I will remember myself. Detached and at ease, I will dart past the Eagle to be free."

WARRIOR-HUMBLENESS-[THE WARRIORS' HUMBLENESS]: Warriors seek impeccability in their own eyes and call that humbleness; warriors accept in humbleness both what they are and what power has in store for them; warriors are humbled by their great fortune, the good fortune of having found a challenge.

WARRIOR-IMPECCABILITY-[THE WARRIORS' IMPECCABILITY]: Warriors know that they need energy in order to face the unknown; the action of rechanneling that energy is the warriors' impeccability; warriors re-deploy, in a more intelligent manner, the energy they have and use to perceive the daily world; the only thing that stores energy for warriors is impeccability.

WARRIOR-INTERVENTION-[THE WARRIORS' INTERVENTION]: Warriors know why they must remain reluctant to intervene; the warriors' difficult task of letting others be, of trusting them to be impeccable warriors themselves; the warriors' understanding that acts of conscious intervention are nothing more than arbitrary acts guided by self-interest alone; warriors do not intervene because they do not indulge themselves in the misguided compassion of the average person, they are not so arrogant to wish that everyone be just like themselves.

WARRIOR-INTUITION-[THE WARRIORS' INTUITION]: The warriors' intuition is the activation of the connecting link with intent.

WARRIOR-JOURNEY-DEFINITIVE-[THE WARRIORS' DEFINITIVE JOURNEY]: The warriors' definitive journey is another term for the journey with power to total freedom.

WARRIOR-JOURNEY-RETURN-[THE WARRIORS' JOURNEY OF RETURN]: Warriorship is the warriors' journey of return to the abstract; warriors return victorious to the spirit after having descended into hell.

WARRIOR-JOY-[THE WARRIORS' JOY]: The mood of warriors is a mood of joy; warriors are joyful because they feel humbled by their great fortune, because they are confident of their impeccability, and above all, because they are fully aware of their efficiency; the warriors' joyfulness comes from having accepted that there is no fate, only the promise of power; joy is the ultimate accomplishment of warriors.

WARRIOR-LIGHTNESS-[THE WARRIORS' LIGHTNESS]: Warriors know that they cannot take themselves too seriously; warriors must learn to balance seriousness with lightness and humor; warriors know how to laugh at themselves and behave with the confidence of someone who doesn't have a care in the world.

WARRIOR-LOVE-[THE WARRIORS' LOVE]: Love has many meanings for warriors; the great unconditional love of warriors is their love of this earth, this world; unconditional love is one of the bridges between the great contradictions of the warriors' world; the warriors' conditional feelings of love are part of the boundaries that human feelings create around things of this world; the warriors' unconditional love grows out of a detachment from the first attention and it's agendas.

WARRIOR-PATIENCE-[THE WARRIORS' PATIENCE]: Warriors are never idle and never in a hurry; warriors wait patiently because they know that they are waiting and they know what they are waiting for; warriors have only their will and their patience, and with them they build anything they want.

WARRIOR-PEACE-[PEACE FOR THE WARRIOR]: Peace is an anomaly for warriors; warriors find peace while they wage a never-ending war, a total struggle against the individual self that has deprived them of their power; as a result of being impeccable, warriors find peace, satisfaction and attainment in a victory without glory or reward.

WARRIOR-PREDILECTION-[THE WARRIORS' PREDILECTION]: The warriors' connection with the abstract is an innermost predilection; this predilection expresses itself in many ways, including the warriors' love for the earth and the fact that warriors "have to believe"; warriors have certain personal issues which press them the most; these are unbiased reactions to the warriors' lot in life; warriors accept their predilections and say, "So be it!"

WARRIOR-PROACTIVITY-[THE WARRIORS' PROACTIVITY]: The warriors' proactivity is the magical stance that positions warriors to flow with power instead of against it; warriors are proactive, they allow themselves to flow with power through their impeccable actions and attitude.

WARRIOR-SOBRIETY-[THE WARRIORS' SOBRIETY]: The warriors' sobriety is the warriors' internal strength, a sense of equanimity, a feeling of being at ease; sobriety is a profound bent for examination and understanding; sobriety is ruthlessness, the opposite of self-pity and self-importance; sobriety is a position of the assemblage point.

WARRIOR-SOLIDITY-[THE WARRIORS' SOLIDITY]: Warriors know that until they have conserved enough energy to withstand the onslaughts of the nagual, encounters with the unknown weaken them and open their gaps; warriors can also solidify themselves using anything else that connects them to the first attention and its inventory.

WARRIOR-STRATEGY-[THE WARRIORS' STRATEGY]: Life for warriors is an exercise in strategy; warriors set their lives strategically and battle to the very end; warriors fight self-importance as a matter of strategy.

WARRIOR-WAR-[WAR FOR THE WARRIOR]: War is the natural state for warriors; war for warriors is the total struggle against the individual self that has deprived us of our power; warriors go to knowledge as they go to war, wide-awake, with fear, with respect, and with absolute assurance.

WARRIOR-WAY-[THE WARRIORS' WAY]: The warriors' way is the way of the impeccable action, sometimes called the sorcerers' way; to be a warrior is a more suitable way of life than anything else.

WARRIORSHIP-[WARRIORSHIP]: Warriorship is the individual attempt to reestablish the link with intent and regain the use of it without succumbing to it.

WILL-[WILL]: Warriors know that will is the mysterious force that is present throughout everything there is; will is the force that keeps the Eagle's

196 • *CREATIVE VICTORY*

emanations separated and is not only responsible for awareness but also for everything in the universe; will is the energy of alignment; will accounts for the perception of the ordinary world and indirectly, through the force of that perception, it accounts for the placement of the assemblage point in its customary position.

WORDS-FLAW-[THE FLAW WITH WORDS]: Warriors know that the flaw with words is that they force us to feel enlightened even though we are not; enlightenment is a result of the acquisition of true knowledge, a process that occurs independent of language all together.

WORLD-MYSTERIOUS-[THE MYSTERIOUS WORLD]: Warriors know that the world is an unknown and marvelous place which exists far beyond the capacities of conscious reason and understanding; warriors respect the incomprehensible nature of the universe and are humble in the midst of it.

WORLD-SOLID-OBJECTS-[THE WORLD OF SOLID OBJECTS]:
Warriors are aware that the world of solid objects is only a way of making our passage on earth more convenient; it is only a description that was created to help us; the solidity of the perceivable world is no more than the force of alignment; certain emanations are routinely aligned because of the fixation of the assemblage point on one specific spot, and that is all there really is to our world.

RECOMMENDED READING

For readers interested in learning more about nagualism and the Toltec warriors' dialogue, the following books are highly recommended:

Tomas. *The Promise of Power: Reflections on the Toltec Warriors' Dialogue from the Collected Works of Carlos Castaneda,* Norfolk, VA: Hampton Roads Publishing, 1995. The author's concordance to the Toltec warriors' dialogue (the nine published works of Carlos Castaneda). This reference guide contains over 5,000 terms and 10,000 individual references, making it an invaluable informational and intuitive directory to the written record of nagualism and the teachings of don Juan.

Castaneda, Carlos. *The Teachings of Don Juan: A Yaqui Way of Knowledge.* New York: Simon and Schuster, 1968. The first book of the Toltec warriors' dialogue.

Castaneda, Carlos. *A Separate Reality: Further Conversations with Don Juan.* New York: simon and Schuster, 1971. The second book of the Toltec warriors' dialogue.

Castaneda, Carlos. *Journey to Ixtlan: The Lessons of Don Juan.* New York: Simon and Schuster, 1972. The third book of the Toltec warriors' dialogue.

Castaneda, Carlos. *Tales of Power.* New York: Simon and Schuster, 1974. The fourth book of the Toltec warriors' dialogue.

Castaneda, Carlos. *The Second Ring of Power.* New York: Simon and Schuster, 1977. The fifth book of the Toltec warriors' dialogue.

Castaneda, Carlos. *The Eagle's Gift.* New York: Simon and Schuster, 1981. The sixth book of the Toltec warriors' dialogue.

Castaneda, Carlos. *The Fire From Within.* New York: Simon and Schuster, 1984. The seventh book of the Toltec warriors' dialogue.

Castaneda, Carlos. *The Power of Silence.* New York: Simon and Schuster, 1987. The eighth book of the Toltec warriors' dialogue.

Castaneda, Carlos. *The Art of Dreaming.* New York: HarperCollins, 1993. The ninth book of the Toltec warriors' dialogue.

Abelar, Taisha. *The Sorcerers' Crossing: A Woman's Journey.* New York: Viking Penguin, 1992. A stalker's account of her initiation into the world of sorcery.

Donner, Florinda. *Being-In-Dreaming: An Initiation into the Sorcerers' World.* New York: HarperCollins, 1991. A dreamer's account of her initiation into the world of sorcery.